# Captivated

By Nicole Edwards (cont.)

**The Devil's Playground Series**

Without Regret

**The Pier 70 Series**

Reckless

**The Sniper 1 Security Series**

Wait for Morning

Never Say Never

**The Southern Boy Mafia Series**

Beautifully Brutal

Beautifully Loyal

**Standalone Novels**

A Million Tiny Pieces

Inked on Paper

**Writing as Timberlyn Scott**

Unhinged

Unraveling

Chaos

**Holiday Books**

2015

*Club Destiny*
Book 4.5

# Nicole Edwards

Nicole Edwards Limited
PO Box 806
Hutto, Texas 78634
www.NicoleEdwardsLimited.com
www.slipublishing.com

**Captivated**: *A Club Destiny Novella* is a work of fiction. Names, characters, businesses, places, events and incidents are either the products of the author's imagination or used in a fictitious manner. Any resemblance to actual persons, living or dead, or actual events is purely coincidental.

Cover Images: © *moodboard | Corbis (42-20559009)*

Interior Images: © *ussr | 123rf.com (31898688)*

Cover Design: Nicole Edwards Limited

Editing: Blue Otter Editing **www.blueotterediting.com**

ISBN (ebook): 978-1-939786-06-7
ISBN (print): 978-1-939786-05-0

Erotic Romance
Mature Audience

# Table of Contents

# Dedication

To all of the ladies who put a smile on my face, day after day.
You know who you are.

Much love,
Nicole

# *Prologue*

"LUCIE, I SURE as hell hope you know what you're doing."

Yes, she was talking to herself. *Again.*

Lucie Werner walked into the small restaurant close to the club where she worked, glancing around to see whether he'd gotten there first. From what she could tell, Kane wasn't there, which was just fine by her. She needed a few minutes to figure out a plan. Well, not really a plan. More like the words to explain the horrible, deceitful secret she'd been keeping from him for so long.

Taking a seat in the back, Lucie was grateful that the place wasn't busy. At three o'clock in the afternoon, she'd been banking on missing the lunch crowd. Considering she had selected this place because it was public, hoping Kane might take that into consideration before he lost his cool, which she knew, for an absolute fact, he was going to do.

When he walked through the front doors a moment later, Lucie suddenly felt sick. Really, really sick. She peered through the restaurant, trying to locate the bathrooms in the event that her stomach decided to revolt against her thanks to those irritating little things called nerves.

"Lucie," Kane greeted her, taking a seat across from her as he glanced around the restaurant as though expecting someone else to show up and save him.

Nope. Not today. Today it was just her.

"Thanks for coming," she said, but she had to clear her throat just to get the words out.

"Is everything okay?"

The concerned look in Kane's eyes was nearly her undoing. If he only knew what she had to tell him, he wouldn't be looking at her as though he were worried about her health.

"No." That was a sad truth. Everything was not okay, nor was she sure it ever would be again.

"What's going on, Lucie?"

Lucie detected his frustration level rising, which was not all that unusual for Kane. He wasn't a patient man by any means. And since she hadn't told him what she wanted to talk about when she'd called him earlier, she knew his curiosity was probably getting the best of him.

"I need to talk to you," she choked out, looking around for the waitress. She needed a glass of water or something. Her throat was constricted by the tears she'd been shedding for the better part of the last day and a half. Ever since she'd made the decision to tell him.

When Kane reached out and touched her hand, Lucie immediately jerked away from him as though he'd shocked her. She couldn't touch him. No matter how badly she wanted to. In a few minutes, she was pretty sure he'd never want to lay eyes on her again, so this only made it easier.

*Fuck that.* There wasn't anything easy about this as far as she was concerned.

"Lucie." Kane's tone went from friendly to stern, and she knew she was just wasting time.

"I need to talk to you about Haley," she began, feeling the tears returning with a vengeance.

"Luke already told me," Kane responded before she could continue.

"He *what?*" How could Luke do that to her? Why would he? And why hadn't Kane come to talk to her?

"Luke told me that he caught you stealing liquor. But he told me that it's all been taken care of. He understands why you did it."

*Oh, God.* That certainly wasn't what she wanted to tell him, but the fact that Kane didn't hate her for that alone was promising. Yes, she'd been stealing liquor from Luke McCoy, the owner of the club she worked for, but she'd had a good reason. Well, it made sense in her mind. Except, sort of like everything else, it really didn't make any sense; she'd just pretended it did.

When she had found out that Haley needed to have surgery because of her chronic illnesses, she'd been desperate. On her salary, she could barely afford the apartment she and Haley lived in, much less the amount of money the doctors told her it would cost to get Haley well.

But that wasn't why she was here. She needed to focus. To tell Kane exactly what she'd been keeping from him for the last five years.

"That's not what I want to tell you," she whispered, unable to stop the first of the tears from breaking free.

"Lucie, you're scaring me. What's going on?" Kane asked her again, but this time he didn't sound concerned. He sounded angry.

"My daughter, Haley"—Lucie swallowed hard, but continued—"she's your daughter."

KANE DIDN'T MOVE.

He couldn't say a word. Hell, he would be surprised if he was even breathing.

Staring back at Lucie, he tried to process what she was telling him, but there was absolutely no fucking way he had heard her right. There was no way that her daughter, who was now four years old, could belong to him.

Absolutely no way.

In case Lucie didn't know, two people had to have sex in order for that to happen, and he sure as hell knew he'd never had sex with her, because if he had, he would fucking remember it.

Leaning back in his chair, Kane dropped his hands into his lap and stared back at her. She was crying, and his first thought was that he'd missed something vitally important. His second thought was that she was totally out of her fucking mind.

"Want to run that by me again?" Kane asked the question when he finally found his voice. He didn't even sound like himself.

"Haley is your daughter," she repeated, sounding as though she believed what she was saying.

Kane couldn't believe his ears, but there was something in the back of his mind that told him she wasn't out-of-her-mind delirious. For years, Kane had felt like he and Lucie had a connection, although, for the life of him, he had no idea why he felt that way. Sure, he was attracted to her. Lucie was a beautiful woman. But that was as far as it went.

"It's not possible," he barked, the fury beginning to churn in his gut. She was lying to him. Why the hell would she do that?

"It's true." Lucie was sobbing almost uncontrollably now, and Kane had no idea why she was crying.

"When? How?" Okay, now that sounded stupid because he knew how babies were conceived, but he just could not figure out how he factored into this.

"I drove you home from the bar one night after we'd all stayed late. You'd been drinking shots, and you were in no condition to drive. You invited me in your house."

Kane heard her words, but he didn't know what she was talking about. She had to be delusional. There was no other way to explain it. Kane would've remembered. He couldn't have been that...

*Oh, shit.*

Kane was having a hard time breathing again.

Haley was four years old. That meant she was conceived nearly five years ago. That was the year... No. No, no, no. He hadn't.

Staring back at her blankly, Kane said the only thing he could say. "I want a paternity test."

"Absolutely," Lucie agreed easily, wiping her eyes with a napkin she'd taken from the table as Kane watched her. "I'll pay for it. I'm so sorry, Kane. So very, very sorry."

With the blood crashing in his ears, Kane could barely make out the words Lucie was saying. He couldn't believe... It had to be a mistake...

Kane blinked, his vision hazy for a second before it cleared. Staring back at the dark-haired woman sitting across from him, he suddenly realized she was telling him the truth. He couldn't remember, but he knew without a doubt that Lucie Werner wasn't lying to him. He had no idea why he believed her, but he did. And she'd agreed to a paternity test, which would prove it. He needed proof. He'd get proof.

He wasn't sure whether he'd be able to stand up and walk out of the restaurant, but he knew three things for absolute certain: He had slept with Lucie and Haley was his daughter. He didn't remember a fucking thing about that night. And Lucie had been keeping him from his daughter all this time.

Now, if only the red haze would fade from his vision and he could manage not to wrap his fingers around Lucie's neck and squeeze the life out of her, Kane might just be able to figure out what to do next.

# Chapter *One*

*Six months later...*

STANDING BEHIND THE long edge of the bar, Kane Steele watched as his boss descended the stairs from the second floor. If he'd thought a shitty day couldn't get worse, he hadn't considered the fact that Luke McCoy had been in rare form for the better half of the night.

"Kane!" Luke's powerful voice boomed from across the room and raked like fingernails down a chalkboard across Kane's last nerve.

It was the end of the night — or rather, morning — for crying out loud. Didn't the man have something better to do? Or better yet — *someone* ... no, make that *two someones* to do?

"What's up?" Doing his best not to sound frustrated, Kane pasted on what would pass as a smile and turned his attention to the imposing man making his way across the now empty club floor.

Call him a pessimist, but after having spent the last few nights watching all of the happy fucking people wandering around the bar — namely the McCoy clan, who'd been congregating at Club Destiny in celebration of one thing or another it seemed for weeks now — Kane wasn't finding it easy to be in a good mood these days.

The fact that Luke had thought it funny to introduce karaoke night to the already rowdy crowd hadn't helped, either. If he had to listen to another garbled rendition of one of Adele's songs, he'd be inclined to gouge his own ears.

Okay, so Kane doubted he would win any awards for his personality, and to his credit, he made a point not to walk around pissed off — or he tried to, anyway. If he were being scored for his optimistic outlook, sure, the results would be subpar, but at least he'd have some points. Maybe.

He was having one hell of a time finding much to be optimistic about lately. Unless, of course, someone mentioned his daughter, then the smile was genuine.

"Why are you still here?"

*Because you're hollering my name, maybe?*

Kane wasn't about to voice his thoughts, but that's what dashed through his brain as he stared at Luke from across the pristine bar top. As a matter of fact, he had just finished up the last of his inventory count for the night, he'd checked to make sure everything was clean and ready for the next night, and was planning to head out, but it appeared that might be changing.

"I'm finishing up," he offered, his gaze landing on the woman walking across the room at a fast clip.

Trying to get away, was she?

"Lucie!" Kane called out, leaning to the right so that he could see around Luke's massive frame.

He fully expected Lucie to continue walking right out the door and ignore him altogether, so when she stopped suddenly, he bit back a grin. At least she was getting better about tolerating him. At least in public. Then again, maybe she just didn't want to cause a scene with Luke present.

Lucie Werner was the bane of his existence. He wanted to both hate her and love her at the same time. Oh, what a difference the last six months had made, though. What with all of the drama with Club Destiny and the McCoys, Kane hadn't had much time to dwell on what was or wasn't going on between him and Lucie at the moment.

Ever since Lucie's admission that Kane was, in fact, the father of her daughter, he'd been eaten up with both guilt and anger, and unable to explain the reason for the former.

Initially, right after Lucie had shared her earth-shattering news, Kane had been livid. He could hardly stand to look at her; he had been so fucking mad that she would've kept something like that from him. He'd insisted on a paternity test and successfully managed to treat Lucie like the scum of the earth.

Now, well... Now things were different.

Sort of.

For the last few months, Kane had spent the majority of his time with both Haley and Lucie and found that if he had a choice, he wouldn't be anywhere else. Even on the days that Lucie allowed him to take Haley to do something on his own, he found he wished she were right there with them. For some reason, he just felt complete with her there.

Explain that one!

Although he had always sensed that something had actually happened between him and the beautiful woman now turning to face him with a scowl on her face, Kane had chalked it up to an overactive imagination, and an even stronger desperation to fuck her. As it turned out, all of those images that had been flashing through his brain for months hadn't been dreams as he'd originally thought. No, he was pretty sure they were suppressed memories coming back to torment him.

According to Lucie, those images were real, at least according to the way she'd described in very high-level detail what had happened between them. He'd just somehow managed to do what he had longed to do without as much as a single conscious memory of it.

Which sucked like hell.

How could he have fallen into bed with Lucie and not remembered a damn thing?

The alcohol was undoubtedly a monumental factor in his memory loss that night. He'd had more than his fair share and rightfully so. That had been a rough time for him, and obviously taking advantage of Lucie had topped off a really awful period in his life.

Since then, after she'd spilled her news and he'd gotten past the blinding rage, things had gotten somewhat easier, for him at least. Not that he could say the same for Lucie. She'd gone from having a baby without a father, which he could only imagine was hard as hell to manage on her own, to having to figure out what the best way to include him was.

While her life was getting significantly more difficult, Kane had been working hard to right the wrongs of their past as best he could. He didn't think Lucie cared much for his interference, but he admired her patience. She certainly had more than he did.

"Are you heading home?" Kane asked as he moved out from behind the bar, leaving Luke behind. It wasn't that he was purposely ignoring his boss, but at the moment, Lucie was more important.

"Yes. Haley's at home with Erica, and I need to get there as soon as possible."

Kane had met Erica, Haley's nighttime babysitter, only a few times. Being a complete and utter jackass, thanks to his original disbelief and anger, he'd actually questioned Lucie at length about the woman. Lucie had assured him — with the patience of a damn saint — that Erica was one of the best things to have ever happened to Haley. Now that Kane knew her, he couldn't disagree. The twenty-two-year-old college student watched Haley from the time Lucie left for work until she walked through her door in the wee hours of the morning.

In all fairness, Kane had never been a hard-ass when it came to his employees, especially those with children. He always tried to ensure that they never had to stay later than the normal closing time if at all possible. Although he had grown a bit protective of Lucie in recent months, he still tried to ensure he didn't show her any preferential treatment.

Well, except for the fact that he wanted to ensure she made it home, as well. Which was why he'd resorted to catching her on her way out, just to remind her that he expected a phone call to let him know she made it home safely.

"Call me when you get there," he told her, locking his eyes with hers and daring her to argue with him.

Interestingly enough, she had only argued one time, and that had been the first time he'd insisted, which he knew had taken her by surprise. She had called him heavy-handed, and he had all but laughed it off. Okay, so maybe that was partly true.

At least since then, Lucie had stopped being so standoffish with him, but he definitely would not consider her warm when it came to their interactions.

"Okay," Lucie said abruptly, then turned and made a beeline for the back doors that led to the parking garage. Little did Lucie know, but Kane would watch her until she was in her car and on her way out of the parking garage. He figured she certainly wouldn't have taken too kindly to that, so he'd managed to hide it for the last few weeks.

Five minutes later, after he'd ensured that she was safely on her way, he pulled out his cell phone, made sure the ringer was on before sliding it back in his pocket. Fifteen minutes, tops. That's how long it would take her to get home, and like clockwork, she had always called. Even though she didn't linger on the phone, Kane still felt better knowing she was safe.

The impatient part of him wished they could gloss over all of the anger and pain that they'd caused each other in recent months, but he knew that was easier said than done. Mending what was broken between them was going to take time, even if he didn't like it.

At least he could say that there weren't any issues currently between him and his beautiful daughter, Haley. He'd taken baby steps with her, reaching out to a counselor from the very beginning to help them through the transition. Lucie had refused to go with them, but Kane couldn't necessarily blame her. But he was happy to say Haley was warming up to him much faster than he'd ever imagined, even if her mother was keeping her distance.

He was hoping he could change that, because, despite her deceit, Kane knew Lucie, and he knew she was only trying to do what was best for everyone involved. Well, except for herself. She never had been one to put herself first. But she had tried to make the best out of a bad situation, and he truly believed she'd thought keeping Haley's paternity from him was the best thing for both Haley and Kane.

He obviously didn't agree, but that was in the past now, and they had so much to work out. It was just going to take some time.

LUCIE HURRIED TO her car, feeling the heat of Kane's gaze burning a hole in her back as he tracked her through the parking garage. A single woman made sure she knew her surroundings, and Lucie had felt his presence since the very first time he'd watched her leave.

Hell, she knew every single time the man so much as glanced her way because she could feel the warmth of his gaze like a physical caress. No matter how much distance she tried to put between herself and Kane, Lucie had a damn hard time getting him off of her mind. It wasn't like anything had changed in that regard, though, even after recent events. She'd felt that way ever since that fateful night five years ago when she'd easily fallen for the man in the span of just a few hours, only to find out he didn't remember a single minute of it.

Before she'd done the unthinkable.

Looking back on it now, Lucie knew that keeping Haley's paternity a secret from her father wasn't the brightest move she'd ever made, and she didn't need a damn psychologist to confirm that, either.

It also didn't change the fact that she still stood by her belief that it'd been the right thing to do.

At the time.

She also knew that no one else agreed with her. Not her mother, not Cole, the one friend who had stood by her the entire time, and especially not Kane.

Had she not gone into complete and total panic over her daughter's chronic health issues, Lucie probably would have never dropped a bomb on Kane, either. Had she ever decided to tell him on her own, she knew she wouldn't have chosen those circumstances as her reason.

He'd been understandably furious, and Lucie couldn't blame him at all. She'd somehow managed to hold herself together after he'd ranted and raved and called her every vile name he could think of all while telling herself that she deserved every bit of his hatred.

When he'd insisted on a paternity test, Lucie had offered to pay for it. He had refused her that, though, and she realized that Kane knew full well Haley was his, but he had to go through the motions. It had hurt to see how he looked at her with such disdain, but Lucie saw the same expression every time she looked in the mirror. She was more disappointed in herself than anyone else ever could be.

Seeing Haley's recent changes, after the surgeries to help her to get over the chronic strep throat and ear infections, as well as her recent interaction with her father, Lucie was in a different place.

Admitting you were wrong was hard enough. Admitting you were wrong about something that altered the course of so many people's lives was even worse. Knowing she was the only reason Haley and Kane had missed out on so many wonderful milestones together had Lucie riddled with guilt.

Not that Lucie could have been convinced otherwise, even when she'd resorted to stealing from Club Destiny just to try and come up with the money to pay for Haley's medical bills. Thankfully, Luke wasn't the complete and total hard-ass everyone said he was. Or maybe he'd just been easy on her because he was in love with Cole, a man who had stood by Lucie through some extremely dark times, one of the only people she could call a friend.

But right now, just like back then, there was no room in her thoughts for Kane Steele and the *what might've beens* that plagued her on a daily basis. She had a job that she needed to focus on and a daughter to care for — and not a second extra to spend on anything more than that.

Ten minutes later, Lucie was turning into her apartment complex, surveying the dark corners of the parking lot and the hidden nooks and crannies of the dilapidated building she lived in. Unfortunately, she had learned the hard way just what lurked in the dark of the night in the less-than-stellar neighborhood. She'd been lucky that night, she knew. Armed with only her car keys, Lucie had managed to fend off her attacker at three o'clock in the morning, when not a single soul had answered her cries for help.

Now she was paranoid, and rightfully so. She hadn't told anyone. Not the police, not her mother, and certainly not Kane. She had too many people trying to look after her as it was. She also feared that Kane would try to take her baby girl away from her if he knew, which meant she only had one option. Be prepared in order to ensure it didn't happen again and continue saving money until she could move to a better neighborhood. She was so close, but that didn't make getting out of her car any easier.

There was one bright side to the whole situation, and that was that Lucie had found Erica, Haley's full-time babysitter. The woman was Heaven-sent, in Lucie's opinion.

Each night, Erica graciously brought Haley back to the apartment — before dark — just to make sure the little girl got to go to sleep in her own bed. And when Lucie arrived at three or four o'clock in the morning, Erica would sometimes remain on the couch, or she would drag herself home if she had an early class. On those nights, Lucie would lock Haley inside the apartment and then dutifully walk Erica to her car just to ensure her safety.

Of course, there were days like yesterday when Lucie would take Haley to Erica's and the little girl asked if Kane would be coming over to see her. Never did Lucie know for sure whether he was, but his track record over the last few months pretty much allowed Lucie to ensure Haley that he would. Kane did little else other than visit his daughter each and every day.

Since they both worked until two in the morning, or later, he didn't get to see Haley in the evenings, but he made sure he was over each day, either bringing lunch to them or taking them somewhere — usually McDonald's if Haley had her say.

Although their interactions were awkward at best, Lucie and Kane managed to be civil to one another when Haley was within earshot. Not that he had talked to Lucie much any other time, but she knew the day would come. He had some big questions he wanted answers to, and she was trying to avoid that conversation like the plague. Even after her high-level account of what had happened, she knew Kane wasn't satisfied with her answers.

Hurrying up the stairs to the second-floor landing, Lucie approached with her keys ready. As was her routine, she had both of the locks unlocked, herself inside, and the reverse completed within seconds. With her phone at the ready, she hit the call button, dialing Kane's number and then waiting for him to answer.

"Everything okay?" Without fail, he asked the same question he asked every time she called.

"Yes. I'm here and Haley's sleeping."

"Okay. I'll see you in a few hours."

Lucie hung up and wondered if that would be the extent of their conversations from here on out. Each day, she hoped for minimal interaction with the man because, despite the relationship he was building with Haley and his ability to at least look her in the eye these days, Lucie had a difficult time getting over the attraction she still felt for him. It seemed to burn hotter and brighter every time she was close to him.

It wouldn't be so terrible if she thought there might be a chance in hell of them ever replaying that one spectacular night all over again. Or better yet, if she thought there was even a remote chance he might feel a fraction of what she felt for him. Despite the repeated lectures she gave herself, it all boiled down to the fact that Lucie was still in love with Kane.

There was no doubt in her mind that Kane would never be able to forgive her completely for what she did. Nor would he ever be able to truly trust her. And that meant these feelings that she had for him were better left tucked away, deep down, and God help her, if she were lucky, eventually forgotten.

# Chapter *Two*

*Three months later...*

THREE O'CLOCK COULD not have come fast enough for Kane. He'd been anticipating this morning for the last week, and now that it was here, he was admittedly feeling a little nervous.

With Haley at Lucie's mother's house for the next few days, Kane knew it was time for him to seize the opportunity. Because Lucie wouldn't have any excuses, he was looking forward to getting some things hashed out between them. The tiptoeing around, avoiding eye contact, and otherwise ignoring one another was seriously beginning to piss him off.

Although he went to see Haley every single day because he was so enthralled by the miracle that was his daughter, Kane and Lucie didn't seem to be making any headway. In fact, she seemed to be pulling away more and more each time he tried to get closer. That was mostly his fault, he knew. Ever since that creep Justin Jones had come into the picture about a month ago, Kane hadn't been able to be around Lucie without getting pissed off.

Maybe he didn't have the right to tell her whom she could and could not date, but Kane didn't like the little shit who had been stalking her at least three or four nights a week at the club one bit. He had to hand it to Lucie; she handled him fairly well. Kane wasn't entirely convinced they were actually dating, but he still felt the need to interfere anytime the opportunity presented itself.

Kane knew Lucie was extremely careful with Haley — probably a tad on the paranoid side, in fact. And as far as he knew, Justin had never even been introduced to his little girl. If he had anything to say about it, he never would, either.

Admittedly, it had taken a little while for him to get past the initial anger and resentment of Lucie's deceit, but now that he was, Kane was beginning to think about things he knew he shouldn't. Like getting Lucie in his bed — or hers — he didn't care either way. The fact that she hadn't dated another man, as far as he knew, for the last few years probably hadn't helped him, either. The problem was, he'd been stupid enough to hold back because he hadn't had any real motivation to pursue her. Until now.

Since he couldn't clearly remember anything about that one night so long ago when he'd obviously taken what he had wanted for so long, Kane was anxious to go back there. Only this time without the alcohol impairing him.

Even without the memories, each time he was close to Lucie, he got the sense of what her skin would feel like beneath his fingertips. It was quite possible that his subconscious remembered her, the feel of her soft, smooth skin, the taste of her sweet mouth, but he wasn't satisfied with almost knowing. He was ready to experience all of those things again, and those were the G-rated visions he had about her. His cock wasn't able to decipher between real and make-believe, so those fleeting images that came out of nowhere to fuck with his mind had a damn near painful effect on him.

Unable to remember anything they'd done that night, he couldn't help imagining what it would feel like to have his cock buried in her sassy mouth, or sliding between her better-than-perfect tits, or deep in her pussy while he made her scream his name as she came. Or better yet, buried to the hilt in her ass while he gripped her hair in his fist, taking her in ways he'd only ever dreamed about.

Kane wasn't a gentle lover, never had been, nor did he feel the need to pretend he was. His desire was ferocious, his urges brutal, and all of his desire had been aimed at Lucie for as long as he could remember. Now he just had to find a way to satisfy his craving for this woman once and for all.

And Kane was sure as shit not about to let some young punk come in and intrude on what he wanted more than his next breath.

"You going home?" Kane asked when Lucie tried to walk past him without as much as a good-bye.

He hadn't seen Justin in the club all night, and he only could hope she didn't have any plans with the man now that Haley would be at her mother's for a few days. If she didn't plan to go home, her plans were about to change.

"Yes, and I know the drill now, Kane. I'll call you as soon as I get there." Her tone was guarded, her eyes filled with irritation.

"I'm coming by," he informed her, and he hoped she heard the lack of request in his tone. He wasn't asking permission.

"Haley's not there. She's at my mother's."

"I know," Kane replied. "That's why I'm coming by. We need to talk."

Lucie eyed him suspiciously for a minute, maybe two, before she shook her head, telling him no. "I'm too tired right now. Can we do this tomorrow?"

"No." That was his final answer. Kane wasn't putting this off any longer. They didn't have to talk if she didn't want to, but he was still going to her house. Whatever this was that he felt for her, he was almost certain she felt it, too. Since this was the perfect opportunity to test the waters, he wasn't going to back down on this one.

"I'll be there in half an hour," Kane said. "I've got to finish up here."

"Kane, I don't—"

Before Lucie could come up with any more excuses, Kane pressed up against her, eliminating all of the space that had been separating them. He placed his finger on her lips to shut her up, although he'd have much preferred to use his mouth, but he was cognizant of where they were. "I'm coming over. You better be there when I get there."

Rolling her eyes and sighing deeply, Lucie nodded her head briefly, then spun on her heel and walked away.

He knew she recognized the frustration in his tone, but he was willing to bet she didn't realize every ounce of it was sexual in nature and he was past the point of waiting for her to come around.

It was time they got some things cleared up — including those damn memories that still eluded him.

DRIVING HOME IN the dark hours of the early morning, Lucie wondered whether the pounding of her heart was actually the first signs of a heart attack. Ever since Kane had mentioned that he was coming by, she'd been feeling strange. Between the constant thump of her heart against her ribs and the roar of blood in her ears, she was beginning to get a little worried.

Kane's words reverberated back and forth in her head, leaving her wondering whether she had heard him correctly. Not the words necessarily but the way he'd said them. He'd thrown her off-balance with his domineering attitude, but even more so when he'd pressed his finger to her lips.

For a second there, Lucie hadn't known whether her knees were going to hold her upright. She wanted to believe that the hunger she'd detected in his words was real, but she was worried her overactive imagination might just be getting the better of her. After all, she hadn't been sleeping well for a few months now, so it was quite possible.

Until recently, when Kane had begun shooting daggers from his eyes whenever Justin Jones would come visit her at the club, he had been totally indifferent to her. Or at least she thought he had been.

His interference hadn't been needed, because Lucie had positively no interest in Justin. He continued to ask her out; she continued to turn him down. Since Haley was her first and foremost priority, Lucie didn't give a second thought to dating a man who she knew wouldn't be long-term material. Not that she was necessarily looking for long-term, but if anything were to happen, she needed to know that it was at least a possibility.

No matter how many times she thought about those overprotective glances that Kane delivered in her direction, she couldn't wrap her mind around any reason. Well, other than him wanting to ensure that his daughter always came first. He didn't have anything to worry about there, but she hadn't necessarily explained that to him.

It boggled her mind that she still had the audacity to think Kane might have a slight interest in her. After what she'd done, Lucie was surprised he even chose to speak to her. Even though she secretly wished that there was something between the two of them, she knew better than to get her hopes up.

Even that one night when she'd given herself over to Kane, the night Haley had been conceived, she hadn't been convinced that he'd wanted anything more than sex from her. Considering she didn't have it in her to do casual relationships, it didn't make sense how much she still craved his touch. Especially on those lonely nights when she couldn't get her mind to shut down because it constantly returned to images of the two of them together. Not even touching herself could alleviate the ache that had only intensified over the years.

Thinking back on the night at Club Destiny when she and Kane and a couple of the other bartenders had been sitting around talking had become a frequent occurrence for her lately. She could still remember the feeling that something was wrong with Kane that night. Sticking around to see if he wanted to talk about it had set everything in motion.

He hadn't wanted to talk. Well, not about what was bothering him anyway.

Instead, he'd indulged repeatedly in shots of bourbon as they chitchatted about nothing important until Lucie had finally decided it was time to call it a night. Kane had agreed, but when she'd seen his intention to drive himself home, Lucie had interjected.

That was her first mistake of many that night.

Calling a cab hadn't even been a consideration for her, yet she didn't know why. It was the first thing she thought about when they encountered someone who had overindulged at the club. She remembered thinking that she would never forgive herself if she allowed him to walk out of there and he was hurt or killed, or someone else was, because of his overindulgence. It had taken remarkably little persuading to convince Kane to let her take him home. After forcing him into her car, she'd managed to pry the directions to his house from him before he'd closed his eyes.

She had thought he'd passed out, but when they'd arrived at his house, he'd been immediately awake and talking once more. Her intention had been to let him out at the curb and continue on to her apartment, but that wasn't what had happened. He had seemed a little more alert when his eyes had opened and he'd looked at her, so when he'd asked her to come in, she'd ignored all of those warning bells that had been clanging for the entire drive to his house.

*"Want a drink?" Kane asked as they made it through the front door after he fumbled the keys two or three times.*

*Lucie knew he was past the point of needing another drink, so she passed on his offer but followed him to the kitchen anyway.*

*"No thanks," Lucie answered, feigning interest in her surroundings.*

His house was immaculate, not that she had expected anything less. Kane dressed like a man who had money. He didn't try to make a fashion statement, but his jeans were always expensive, his shirts always trendy and in style. Not to mention, she should've been tipped off as soon as she'd turned into his neighborhood. She had no idea what kind of money he made as the bar manager, but she didn't actually care, either.

As she stood in the kitchen trying to divert her eyes from the sexy-as-hell man standing not two feet away, she began to fidget, suddenly wanting to go home. She shouldn't be there; she knew that much. Not with Kane in his current state of mind, obviously pissed off and now intoxicated as hell.

"I should go," she said, daring to make eye contact with him.

Kane moved closer, and she could smell his sultry cologne, the scent she had dreamed about in the middle of the night. Despite the fact that both of them had that lingering smell of alcohol and cigarettes thanks to working at the bar, Lucie was overwhelmed by the unique scent of him, which overpowered everything else.

"Lucie," Kane whispered as he took two steps closer, suddenly closing the gap between them and effectively backing her up against the granite countertop.

She didn't break eye contact, noticing the way the steel-gray color had darkened, swirling like storm clouds. The single curl that had fallen over his forehead beckoned her fingers to brush it back and then delve into the silken mass to see if it was as soft as it looked.

"Touch me, Lucie," Kane insisted, and for a moment, she wondered if she'd imagined it.

*There wasn't an ounce of gentleness in his tone, strictly fierce hunger and need. It was something she'd come to expect from Kane, but never had she expected him to turn the heat on her.*

*"Touch me, baby," Kane said again, this time with more insistence.*

*Lucie knew she should go, knew she should run out the front door and forget this night had ever happened, but instead she did what she'd longed to do for the past year.*

*Lifting her hand, she placed her trembling fingers against the hard planes of his chest, letting the warmth of his skin penetrate through the soft cotton of his T-shirt. His chest was broad and thick, and Lucie was mesmerized by how small her hands looked in comparison to him.*

*He couldn't have been much more than six feet tall, but she was five foot six, so he still peered down at her. She could feel his heartbeat beneath her palm, and when she looked back up at his eyes, she recognized the same lust burning bright and hot just as it was in her. She knew that if she gave in to this man, he was going to alter her in ways she wasn't entirely sure she would be able to survive.*

Lucie shook off the memory when she pulled into the parking space in front of her apartment. If she'd have known then exactly how much he would change her life, she would have turned and run like she'd wanted to.

Without any additional thoughts about Kane or what the night might bring, Lucie ran to her apartment as she considered her surroundings. By the time she was inside, she was breathless but feeling a little more normal.

As she moved to put her purse on the bar, a knock sounded at her door, and she jumped. *Shit.* Lucie had hoped to at least have a shower before Kane showed up. Without thought, she opened the door, not wanting him to knock again for fear that the noise might disturb her neighbors. She didn't want to give them any reason to hate her.

"You said you would be at the club for another half hour," she huffed in exasperation as she shut the door behind him.

Her apartment wasn't big by any stretch of the imagination, but when Kane walked in, it suddenly felt even smaller.

"I couldn't wait," Kane remarked, making his way into the apartment.

Couldn't wait for what? To come over there and tell her how every decision she'd ever made was the wrong one? Hell, she knew that already, so he wouldn't be telling her anything new.

"For what?" she asked, flipping the deadbolt before turning to face him.

*Oh, hell.*

Looking up into his eyes, Lucie knew her life was about to veer off course yet again.

# Chapter *Three*

KANE STARED DOWN into the chocolate-brown eyes that he'd been dreaming about for the better part of the last six years. Ever since the first time he'd laid eyes on Lucie Werner, he'd been captivated by her delicate beauty. Even more so now than back then.

"To do this." Backing her up against the front door, Kane pressed his body against hers, trying to contain the hunger that pulsed hot and fast through his bloodstream. Cupping her head in his hands, he whispered, "I couldn't wait to put my mouth on you."

Expecting her to move, or even push him away, Kane paused briefly before gently pressing his lips to hers. He had to keep himself grounded in the moment as soon as her soft, warm lips met his, because the inclination to thrust his tongue deep in her mouth was overwhelming.

Her hand lifted to his chest, and he could feel a slight tremor in her fingers and the heat of her skin through his shirt. He had to coax her lips open with his tongue, but her resistance wasn't nearly as strong as he knew she intended.

Once he delved into her mouth, he licked and tasted every soft, succulent inch of her, pressing his body more firmly against hers, aligning his rock-hard cock between her thighs, and grinding like a damn teenage boy who'd just figured out what it meant to have a hard-on.

Damn, she was hot. There was absolutely nothing reserved or timid about this woman when she kissed him.

The urgent scrape of her fingernails against his scalp when she slid her hands into his hair had Kane pulling her closer, growling into the kiss. There was no turning back tonight. Since he couldn't turn back time to relive that moment from years before, it was high time they made some new memories.

After long, drugging kisses, Kane reluctantly pulled his mouth from hers but didn't put any space between them. When their eyes met, Kane knew there wouldn't be any talking tonight. He was confident that's what she'd thought he wanted, and maybe somewhere deep down, he did want to know why she'd thought it best to keep such an enormous secret, but right now, he just needed to feel her. More importantly, he needed Lucie to give herself to him.

"I need a shower," he finally said as he held her close, his palm pressed into her lower back, the other on her hip.

After having been at the bar for fourteen hours, he could smell the revolting stench of cigarette smoke, beer, and the various liquors he'd poured all night. He knew she would be able to smell it on him, too.

"It's down the hall," Lucie stuttered, not breaking eye contact.

"Show me," Kane told her before taking a step back. He fully intended to take a shower, but he didn't plan to do so alone.

Kane could feel Lucie's reluctance; it billowed around her like a lingering cloud undisturbed by the forceful winds churning around them. If he guessed, she was both nervous and anxious, both emotions warring inside of her, and like him, she wasn't sure where this was going. He was going to make the decision for her unless, of course, she told him no.

Kane wanted her with a gut-wrenching passion, but he would never force her. He just couldn't sit back and wait for her to come to him anymore. It was clear she was keeping herself distant, and there was no way in hell he was about to let another man intrude on what he considered his.

When Lucie stopped in front of the bathroom, he took her hand in his and pulled her to him once more. He wasn't letting her get away that easily, and he knew if he left it up to her, she would run and hide from him until he forced her to face the searing heat that they couldn't deny any longer.

Moving her backward until she was in the bathroom with him, Kane shut the door, letting her know his intentions. It was now or never. Either she would succumb to the inferno of lust that ignited when they were in close proximity or she would turn and run. Either way, he was ready to move on to the next phase of what was happening between them.

"Turn on the water, Lucie," he instructed her as he began unbuttoning his shirt.

Watching the emotions play across her face was like watching a deer caught in the headlights of a vehicle moving at a high rate of speed. She wasn't sure what was coming at her, but she knew something was coming, something she couldn't control.

"Kane," she whispered, barely audible even in the small area.

"We can't run from this," he told her, reaching behind her to turn the shower on, because it was obvious she wasn't able to do it based on the way her hands were visibly shaking. "Do you want to run from me, Lucie?"

He wanted to know the answer, but more importantly, he wanted to know the truth. She could deny him all she wanted, but he saw the desire in her penetrating gaze. He'd felt her passion in their kiss, knew she wanted him as much as he wanted her.

"Answer me," Kane ordered, taking a step closer and reaching for the buttons on her shirt. He eased one small disc from its mooring as he kept his eyes locked with hers. The rich chocolate brown swirled, darkening as he continued to undress her one tiny button at a time.

"I'm scared," she whispered.

"Of me?" he asked, suddenly worried about what exactly *had* happened between them all those years ago. Kane could be rough on his lovers; he knew that. And considering that the compelling hunger he harbored for Lucie consumed him, overpowered his senses, he wasn't quite sure what he was capable of. Especially at that moment in time.

"No," she assured him with what sounded like conviction in her tone.

"Then what are you scared of?" Slipping her shirt off of her shoulders, Kane allowed the cotton to glide down her arms, falling to the floor at her feet as he trailed his fingertips down the inside curve of each arm, then back up until he reached the undersides of her breasts.

Glancing down, he watched as her chest expanded with every choppy breath she inhaled, imagining what it would feel like to bite the pebbled tips of her nipples. He didn't give in to the craving yet, though. Instead, Kane let the backs of his fingers graze over her white lace bra before tracing his fingers over her collarbone and then slowly back down. Slipping one finger between her soft skin and her no-nonsense bra, Kane scraped his fingertip over her nipple, moving his eyes up to meet hers.

"What are you scared of?" he repeated, insisting that she answer.

"This," Lucie said, and then released his gaze before turning her attention to where his hand lingered on her breast.

Kane pulled her bra down forcefully, releasing one plump, beautiful globe from the silky confines before he tweaked her nipple with his thumb and forefinger. When Lucie would've thrown her head back, he put his other hand on the back of her head, holding her so she was forced to watch.

"Don't look away," he demanded. "Never look away." The steam from the shower was filling the room, coating her body in a fine sheen of moisture, which only increased his urge to lick her.

Everywhere.

*OH, GOD!* LUCIE wasn't sure she would survive the onslaught of sensation that Kane's brief touched ignited. She was aching for his touch, his kiss, and anything else he could give her.

From the instant he had pressed his lips to hers, her body had caught fire, every nerve ending tingled, begging for the man to do to her what he had done to her so many years ago. She couldn't find her voice, or she would have been begging him, pleading for him to ease the pain that came from wanting him.

When he forced her bra down, Lucie gasped. And when he lowered his head and sucked her nipple into the white-hot depths of his mouth, she cried out, pulling his head closer to her breast as he suckled desperately before easing off and using his tongue to bathe her with intense heat. As she held him to her, she watched, captivated by the sight of his mouth on her skin, the feel of his tongue as it rasped over her hypersensitive nipple.

"Fucking hell," Kane growled, the echo heard through the room and deep in her core, where her womb quivered with need. "You taste so fucking good."

He pulled the other cup of her bra down just as aggressively as the first, releasing her other breast while he pinched her nipple, sending fiery shards of pain ricocheting from her nipple to her clit.

She remembered this about him, remembered how he took what he wanted, making sure to pleasure her along the way, but he never disguised the hunger, the need, and he wasn't gentle. But Lucie didn't want gentle. She wanted Kane — the dominating, controlling man who made her body burn and her senses reel with the ferocity that spiraled through her just from his touch.

He reached around her, his fingers fumbling with the clasp of her bra while he sucked her completely into his molten-hot mouth, before easing back, his teeth gently nipping her painfully erect nipple, sending additional rockets of fiery sensation through her body.

When her bra was finally removed, he took a step back, admiring what he had revealed. And yes, Lucie could see the approval in his stormy gray eyes, and it only intensified her need.

"Take off the rest of your clothes." The words were a demand that left no room for argument. Without hesitation, Lucie found her fingers fumbling on the button of her slacks just as Kane began to do the same on his own, only he didn't seem to be having any issues.

Although it took her longer than him, only a few seconds slipped by before they were both standing completely naked in the steamy bathroom, and Lucie couldn't stop herself from ogling the intensely sexy lines of his body. His chest was broad, each plane of muscle outlined, deliciously defined, as was each ripple of muscle on his stomach. Lucie wanted to spend a few hours outlining those individual slabs with her fingers and her tongue.

He was beautiful.

Kane took her hand, breaking her concentration on his magnificent physique, pulling her into the shower/bath combo before closing the flimsy curtain. The next thing she knew, she was sliding across the slippery tub, her body colliding with his beneath the warm, pelting spray that did nothing to soothe her already overheated skin.

He tilted her head up, using just one finger beneath her chin, his eyes focused on her mouth as he swiped his thumb over her bottom lip before locking his gaze with hers again. "I've dreamed about your mouth on me. I want to feel your lips on my cock, sucking me."

The seductive, raspy pitch of his voice made the words sound even more erotic than they should have. Lucie didn't bother to tell him that he'd spoken almost those same words the last time she had been in his arms, but they had been in his kitchen, not the intimate confines of the shower.

"God, baby." Kane exhaled sharply, pulling her mouth to his, thrusting his tongue past her lips, forcing her to fall into him so she wouldn't fall to the floor. His touch was overwhelming, but his kiss was all-consuming.

When he slid his hands into her hair, pulling her head back and breaking the kiss, she stared up into those stormy gray eyes.

"Suck my cock, Lucie. On your knees, baby," he growled. "I want to feel that sweet mouth on my dick."

The innocent, inexperienced side of her said she should be offended by his crude words, not turned on like she was. They'd been down this road before, only Kane didn't seem to remember it. She did. Vividly. And, truth be told, Lucie wanted to do anything to please him. His dominance appealed to her on a very basic level, and she found she was willing to do exactly as he said.

Kane was demanding, more so than she could have ever imagined, but Lucie felt safe with him. He wouldn't force her; she knew that from experience. He somehow managed to make her want the same things he did just with the deep rumble of his voice and the scorching heat in his eyes. Whatever power he had over her was enough to trigger a maelstrom of energy, bright enough and hot enough to consume her with its intensity.

Lucie lowered herself to her knees, trailing her fingers across the smooth, hairless planes of his chest, letting them slide over the contoured ridges of his abdomen until she was eye level with his beautiful erection. She was eager to touch him, to taste him, to prove in her mind that what had happened all those years ago wasn't a fantasy but a reality that had rocked her to her very core.

It wasn't like she had much experience in the bedroom, or showers, as it were, but based on what she did know, Kane was by far the largest man she'd ever been with, and his cock was in direct proportion with his massive size. Even as she tried, Lucie was unable to encompass the wide shaft with her fingers, but she settled on gently stroking him as best she could, memorizing the velvet-covered steel that pulsed in her hands.

Glancing up at him, she hadn't known what to expect, but the expression on his face hadn't been it. Maybe heat or desire, but not that look of sheer and utter disbelief, as though he couldn't believe they were doing this any more than she could.

His eyes met hers instantly, breaking the vulnerability she had witnessed in his gaze when he twined his fingers in her hair, pulling her to him until the wide crest of his cock brushed her lips. He was hot in her mouth, his fingers rough on her scalp, and she welcomed the sensations because they eased the pain in her knees from being on the hard porcelain of the bathtub.

Being with Kane was like being close to a wild, untamed animal. She didn't know what to expect from him, although she knew from experience the pleasure would be extraordinary. His firm demands and his rough touch spoke to a part of her that she hadn't known existed. The part of her that ached for him, needed him.

"Ahhh, Lucie." Kane groaned as she sucked him in deep, sliding her tongue around the engorged head, then down the underside as he thrust his hips, forcing his thick shaft deeper into her mouth.

She was going to gag; she couldn't help it. He was too large, too thick, but she knew it was what he wanted, for her to take all of him. Since that one night, Lucie had reflected back on the time she'd gone to her knees in his kitchen, the way he'd thrust hard and fast into her mouth, groaning his pleasure as he'd used her just like he was doing now.

She'd longed to taste his saltiness, smell the musky scent of his sex, feel the warm velvet of his cock in her mouth as she eagerly tried to bring him as much pleasure as possible. With eager anticipation, Lucie gave herself over to him, allowing him to push deep, sucking him, licking him, consuming him. Being on her knees was a wickedly hot fantasy that she had never had another opportunity to relive since him.

"So fucking good, baby."

The term of endearment he used had her heart thumping painfully hard in her chest. He'd called her that before, and she wondered if he said as much to all of the women he was with. She hoped not, but with Kane, she knew there had been many women. Many before her and several after.

"Lucie." Her name on his lips spurred her on, forcing her to stop thinking about the pain in her knees or other women he'd been with, making her grip the base of his cock firmly with her hand, slowly stroking him as she continued to pull him into her mouth.

"Take all of me, Lucie," Kane commanded, his hand in her hair pulling tighter.

When he tilted her head back, gripping his own cock and guiding himself deeper, she fought to breathe through her nose, trying desperately not to gag as he pushed deeper than she thought possible.

"Fuck!"

Kane forced himself deep into her throat, retreated before pushing in again while Lucie watched the desperate, hungry expression on his face. He repeated the movements several times before his thigh muscles bunched beneath her hands, and his body stilled. She was met with his salty, warm taste flooding her mouth as he held himself still. Swallowing every last drop, Lucie closed her eyes and relished the fact that she had just made him come with her mouth.

# Chapter *Four*

KANE COULD BARELY stand on his own two feet.

Lucie had robbed him of all his senses, stealing every ounce of his control as she'd eagerly consumed his cock. The way she'd given herself over, eagerly taking him into the liquid-fire depths of her mouth as he'd forced himself deeper had nearly shattered his mind. It wasn't just the feel of her as she deep throated him or those soft moans that had sent sparks shooting up and down his spine. Her trust in him had been humbling, stripping him of all restraint until he was shooting fast and hard down her throat.

Pulling her to her feet now, he pressed her into the tiled wall, trying to gain his equilibrium, because she had tilted his world on its axis, his body and mind floating. Kane had known it would be that way with her, never expecting anything less than mind-numbing bliss, but the other feelings she stirred inside of him were foreign.

From the beginning, Kane had known he wasn't going to use Lucie's body the way he used most of his lovers, giving and receiving only pleasure, but he hadn't expected the sort of intimacy he felt with her, either.

This was something much deeper, more intimate than he had ever expected. Just to think that he didn't remember anything about their first time together still pissed him off. Even if he could blame the booze for his loss of control that night, Kane would give anything to remember what it had felt like.

Looking down into her rich mocha-brown eyes, he cupped her chin, wanting to see the need, because he knew it was there. She'd eagerly consumed him, giving everything and not asking for anything in return. Now he wanted to give her everything. To pleasure her and make her feel the same emotional churn that he was wrought with.

He briefly debated on whether he should fall to his knees and worship her pussy in order to sate her immediate needs, but Kane thought better of it. The shower was too small for what he intended to do, so for now, he'd have to settle on building her need.

Taking a step back, he cupped her face in his hands before pressing his forehead to hers. "You undo me," he whispered, caught off guard by his own admission. Before she realized just how much power she had gained over him, Kane took another step back, ordering her to turn around so that her back was to him.

Reaching for the shampoo bottle sitting on the edge of the tub, Kane filled his palm and proceeded to lather the thick, long strands of her hair, massaging her scalp as he did and feeling his body stir to life when she began to moan again.

"Feel good?"

"Yes," Lucie answered, sounding a little dazed and confused as her body fell back against his.

Once he was finished with her hair, he moved on to her body, using his fingers to learn every graceful curve, every luscious valley of her spectacular body. He took his time exploring her with his fingers, memorizing her smooth, wet skin, inch by inch.

Once he finished teasing her, he quickly washed himself, his cock hardening yet again as he stroked it while Lucie watched. By the time he was done, the water was getting cold, so he turned it off and threw open the shower curtain.

"Towels?" he asked, glancing around the enclosed space.

"In the cabinet," Lucie replied, taking a step back from him. Her voice was husky with arousal, and it only made his cock swell, painfully erect once again. He wasn't even sure how that was possible, but Kane wasn't going to question it.

He opened the cabinet above the toilet and grabbed two towels, tossing one onto the closed toilet seat before he turned back to her and offered his assistance. He admired the rosy pink of her skin from the hot water that had rained down on them. He inhaled the fresh scent of strawberries from her shampoo and was more than ready to lick her to see if she tasted as sweet.

Once he had her dry, he wrapped a towel around her before retrieving the other and drying himself in a rush. Kane was ready to continue making those memories he'd been deprived of the first time he had gotten his hands on her. His cock was fully engaged again and ready to go, but he intended to ravish her in other ways first.

Taking her hand, he pulled her out of the bathroom and back down the hall to the living room. They'd make it to her bedroom before the night was through, but for now, he wasn't going to rush things. Her bed likely would prove to be too much of a temptation, and quite frankly, he'd fantasized a number of times about doing wicked things to her in the only other room in her apartment that he'd ever been in.

Pulling her to him when they were standing in the small space, he unhooked the tab of the towel that was holding it firmly in place over her breasts. To his surprise, she didn't try to hold on to it, rather letting it fall to the floor.

"So pretty." Her skin was flawlessly smooth, a sexy golden brown and so soft to the touch. Using the backs of his fingers, he slid them down the long, sleek column of her neck, over her collarbone, and then down her arm.

"I've waited so long to touch you," he said out loud for the first time. For months, hell, even years, he'd thought them, but never had he put a voice to them. Standing with her, Kane couldn't control the need to tell her exactly what he was thinking, "I might not remember that night, but I've dreamed about it. Dreamed about touching you ... tasting you."

Lucie had had a recurring role in his dreams over the years. Sometimes they were innocent dreams; other times he'd wake up sweating from the heat that he practically could feel generating between them. Even in his dreams, she sparked that flame deep down inside of him. He'd just never been able to come to terms with what he truly wanted from her. More than just sex, he knew. More than even the random pleasantries they shared when he came to see his daughter.

Kane *needed* Lucie.

All of her.

On top of that, he needed to take her, to show her just what was brewing between them, because the physical reaction that his body had to hers defied logic.

Kane eased Lucie down until she was sitting on the edge of the modest wooden coffee table that sat just slightly off-center in the room. Nudging her thighs open with his legs, Kane watched, waited for her to say something. He continued to expect her to put the brakes on, and each second that passed, he wondered whether he'd have the strength to stop if she did.

Lowering himself to his knees, he watched the way her eyes widened and her breaths came faster, but not with fear. He forced her legs open wider with his shoulders, glancing down at the soft, pink folds of her pussy. She was bare, all of the curls gone, just as he had imagined, and he wouldn't be able to get his tongue on her fast enough. Using his hands, he spread her thighs even wider, holding her open as far as he could get her, forcing her to sit up straighter, which allowed her to peer down between her legs to where he began teasing her clit with his tongue.

The taste of her, like moonlight and sunshine swirling together, exploded on his tongue as he teased the swollen little nub while he pushed one finger deep inside her warm, wet heat. It didn't matter how many times he'd dreamt about this moment, or fantasized as he watched her move through the bar, none of those compared to this.

Listening to her sweet moans, feeling her body squeeze his finger, her hips gently rocking as she tried to push his tongue against her clit, was so much better than any dream or any fantasy he'd ever had. And tonight she was all his.

LUCIE WASN'T GOING to last. Her mind was swirling with a mixture of sensations that set her body on rapid boil. She was equally affected by the warmth of Kane's hand on her thigh, the way his tongue rasped against her tender flesh, and the broad finger filling her. He was bombarding her with all of these exquisite touches, relentlessly teasing her until she was hovering dangerously close to the edge. She needed to come, needed to release all of the pent up sexual frustration that had been building without an appropriate release for years. Her own fingers, even her vibrator had never been quite enough. She had always been able to make herself orgasm, but never had it been the same as when she'd been with Kane that one time so many years ago.

He knew how to play her like a well-tuned instrument, and more than anything, Lucie wanted to savor this moment, to make it last as long as she possibly could, but her body had other ideas. She couldn't resist him, couldn't get enough of him. This was Kane, the man she loved without fault, needed beyond reason.

"Kane!" She was so close, yet so far away. Lucie wanted to feel the weight of his body on top of hers, desired to be held in his arms while he lost control the same way she was going to. Just when she thought she would go off like a fireworks display, Kane stopped.

Opening her eyes, she watched as he slowly lifted his head, the heat of his mouth moving up her body, tickling her skin as he pressed damp kisses along her torso, until he sucked one painfully hard nipple into his mouth, making her nearly scream from the pleasure. She needed more. So much more.

"Please."

"Tell me, Lucie," Kane urged as his tongue lashed at her nipple. "Tell me what you want me to do to you."

"Don't stop." That's the only thing she wanted — for him not to stop assaulting her nerve endings with a torturous pleasure.

"I don't plan to stop," he warned, wrapping his arms around her back and pulling her body closer to his. She instinctively wrapped her arms around his neck, cupping the back of his head as she held him close to her breast. It was so good. Painfully good.

Her body was aflame with the desires only this man could bring out in her, and yet she was so close to losing it she could feel the slight quiver in her womb as her orgasm threatened.

"Oh, God, Kane. I need more," she whimpered, and had he been any other man, she would have been mortified. But this was Kane, and even if he didn't remember, she did. She remembered the time he had taken her so roughly just a mere brush of his fingers had set her off. And here she was totally naked in the middle of her living room, wanting nothing more than to feel him inside of her.

"Stand up." He breathed the words against her oversensitive skin as he began pushing to his feet, her arms still wrapped around his neck. "Don't let go of me, Lucie."

Never. She'd never let go if she had anything to say about it. So she kept her arms around his neck and held on as he lifted her in his arms and turned.

When his mouth met hers, she tasted herself on his lips, felt the passion in the way his tongue dueled with hers. If there had been any hesitation on her part initially, it was all gone. Disappearing with the night itself, leaving her open and vulnerable to this one man.

When they reached her bedroom, Lucie expected him to put her on her feet, but instead, Kane lowered her to the bed, coming down on top of her as he did. The blessed weight of his much larger frame against hers crushed her, but it wasn't suffocating her. No, it was the complete opposite. He was grounding her, ensuring she knew exactly where she was and what she was doing.

"Look at me, Lucie." Kane's raspy voice was thick with the same hunger that pulsed through her veins, and Lucie opened her eyes, struck by the deep gray of his eyes swirling with more emotion than just uncomplicated lust.

When Kane pushed himself up with one arm, Lucie watched as the impressive muscles flexed and bunched, his chest hardening even more so than before as he held himself above her.

"Touch me, Lucie," he urged, and Lucie tore her gaze from the strength she'd been admiring to look into his eyes.

What she saw there stole her breath, because even though this could've been only sex between them, she felt as though it was something more. So much more.

Sure, they had a child together, but this wasn't about Haley; this was about the two of them. At this moment, together, exploring one another as though this was the very first time. And for him, maybe it was the first time, but for her... No, she remembered the time before, and that night paled in comparison to this. That night, although she didn't regret one minute, hadn't been laced with this feeling that they were meant to be together.

"I need to be inside of you, Lucie." She heard the urgency in his tone, and her body mirrored the need she could hear in his voice.

Spreading her legs with his knees, Kane eased down closer to her, situating himself between her thighs, but then he moved, glancing around the room as though looking for something.

"What's wrong?" she asked.

"Condom."

Why the idea hadn't even crossed her mind, she didn't know. They didn't need a condom as far as pregnancy went. Not this time. And no, it wasn't because of the fact that they had a child already. It had been stupid on her part to have not used protection the first time they were together, but Lucie had been so overwhelmed that night, so torn up with the emotions that had blinded her, she hadn't even thought about it.

"I'm on the pill," she told him, her eyes meeting his and an unspoken agreement settling between them. "I've been tested, and I'm clean."

After that one night, the night Haley had been conceived, Lucie hadn't been with another man, and yes, she had immediately gone to the doctor to get tested for sexually transmitted diseases because of her own stupidity. And she had routinely been tested after that for a full year. Why she hadn't taken a pregnancy test at that point, she still didn't know.

"I've never..." Kane let the words hang between them, and Lucie suspected he knew what he was about to say was a lie.

He had. They had had unprotected sex that one night so long ago, so what he was about to say wasn't true. She couldn't help but wonder whether it had happened to him on more than one occasion. She didn't want to think about it...

"Except with you, Lucie." Kane leaned in closer, his mouth brushing hers. "I've never had sex without a condom. I swear to you."

She believed him, although she wasn't certain that she should. If anything, Lucie knew Kane would never hurt her intentionally. Even though she had kept Haley's paternity a secret from him, it hadn't been because she'd feared what he would do. She hadn't wanted to trap him, and each night when she'd put her precious little girl to sleep for the last five years, Lucie had prayed Kane would remember, and she would've been relieved of the horrible secret she'd held inside of her.

"I know," she whispered as she pressed farther into him, trying to pull him closer, because that's exactly where she needed him right then.

Kane maneuvered himself until he was between her thighs, the broad, thick head of his penis pressing against the sensitive tissue. She needed him, more now than ever, and she wanted to feel him inside of her again. This time while they were both right there in the moment.

When Kane pressed farther into her, her body relaxed as a sharp burst of pain ricocheted from between her legs, making her whimper.

"Am I hurting you?" he asked, and Lucie met his eyes once more.

"No. Please, Kane." She didn't know how to express what she wanted. Did she beg him to fuck her? Or plead with him to make love to her? This felt like so much more, at least to her. Even the pain was welcome, because she knew it was the only way she could get closer to him.

"Baby..." Kane leaned in, his lips pressing into hers. "God, you feel so good."

Her body consumed him entirely, pulling him deeper as her hands trailed over the rigid, tight muscles of his back, outlining them with her fingertips as tears threatened to spill from her eyes. It was too much.

Finally, when he was seated fully inside of her, Kane began to move, rocking gently against her, pushing himself off of her while she tried to pull him closer. Lucie didn't want him to see the tears in her eyes because it wasn't pain that was causing them. No, they were the result of the love threatening to burst free.

"Lucie." Her name on his lips was like a plea, and their eyes met, held, as he began to thrust inside of her, retreating until her body was begging for more. "Don't let go of me."

He wasn't just speaking of the physical sense; Lucie could feel the emotion in his words, the outpouring of something much more intimate than just his desire to be touched.

"Oh, Kane," she whispered, pulling him closer, trying to close the gap between them until there was no choice but for them to be one. "Please."

"Always, Lucie."

When their bodies took over, her heart took a backseat to the glorious pleasure of having him inside of her, feeling the sensual glide of his penis against greedy nerve endings as he began thrusting harder, her hips rising to meet his.

Lucie was unable to stop the tears from falling, but they weren't what he thought, so she buried her head in the crook of his neck and held him closer, rocking against him as the overwhelming sensations took over, her orgasm spiraling out of control. "Kane! Oh, God, Kane!"

"Fuck, baby." His words were a whisper against her ear as they became one, just like so many years before and so many nights in between in her dreams.

Lucie couldn't get the words out as her orgasm detonated, violent tremors racking her body as she held him close, never wanting this moment to end.

"Lucie. Baby." Kane groaned and then his body stilled, fully seated inside of her. Lucie felt the heated pulse of his cock as his release tore through him.

And if she hadn't known before, Lucie certainly knew now... This man owned her.

Heart and soul.

# Chapter *Five*

"I NEED A week off," Kane told Luke two days later.

He'd hesitated originally, pondering the decision for the last forty-eight hours until he knew exactly what he had to do.

"Okay."

Wondering whether he should get his hearing checked, Kane stared back at Luke, the astonishment on his face probably apparent. For some reason, he had expected an argument, not an immediate acceptance of his request.

"Okay?"

"Were you looking for a different answer?" Luke asked, leaning back in his chair and crossing his arms over his chest.

Shit, he'd expected anything but that. Now came the hard part. "I need Lucie to have a week off, as well. With pay."

A small smile tipped Luke's lips, and Kane had to squint to make sure he saw correctly. Granted, so much had changed with Luke in recent months, but for his hard-ass of a boss to smile was still a little unnerving. "Done."

Luke's easy acceptance threw Kane for a loop, and he couldn't come up with anything to say other than, "Who will cover for us while we're gone?" He'd given it some thought but hadn't come up with a clear plan.

"I think I can get it covered, Kane. I know how to manage my club."

He didn't doubt that, but he also knew that's what Kane was there for. Club Destiny wasn't just a bar, and Luke had his hands full with several other things at the moment, including a high-publicity lawsuit that was taking most of his time, the temporary closing of Club Destiny's doors, not to mention some sort of investment deal he was working on.

"Will you be working tonight?" Luke asked as he leaned forward, resting his arms on the desk and glaring back at Kane.

"Yes." It was Saturday night, and Kane would've never thought of leaving Luke to deal with their busiest night of the week alone, especially not without advance notice.

"All right." Luke smiled again. "When you get back, I need to talk to you about a couple of things. But it can wait, so enjoy your time off."

Kane wasn't sure he liked the sound of that, but what was he going to say? Never mind? *No.* This vacation was more than a little overdue, so it had to come first.

Although he'd received Luke's permission, Kane knew that was the easy part. Now he had to talk to Lucie.

Unfortunately, the talking-to-Lucie part didn't happen as Kane expected. The bar had erupted in chaos only minutes after he'd returned from Luke's office, and he had been going nonstop ever since. Glancing down at his watch as he poured a Belvedere and 7-Up for Samantha McCoy, Kane realized he had several more hours to go, but he needed to talk to Lucie before she tried to sneak out.

Ever since the night he had stayed at her apartment, making love to her again had been the only thing on his mind. Since she seemed to be avoiding him, Kane was bound and determined to ensure they had some time to talk. Not to mention, he was looking forward to spending more than just an hour or two at a time with Haley.

The idea for a vacation had come to him the morning he was leaving Lucie's, which was why he had gone home and immediately gotten on the phone with his travel agent — better known as his mother.

Originally, he'd given some thought to taking Haley and Lucie to Disney World, but being this would be the perfect time for him and Lucie to talk, he figured that might not be the ideal setting for them. When his mother, Susanna, had suggested the beach, Kane had immediately perked to the idea. Having some time with his two girls all to himself sounded just about perfect right now, so he'd instructed his mother to make it happen.

"Hey," Lucie greeted, albeit shyly, when she approached the bar. Kane knew she was just dropping off some drink orders since she was waitressing tonight due to the large number of people, but he was still happy to see her even if it was only briefly. On nights when they were slow, she opted to take over the bar, but on nights like this, it was all they could do to keep up, so he generally had Lucie working the tables.

"Hey." Staring back at the woman, Kane was immediately assaulted by the images of their night together. The night he remembered because it was burned into his brain. "Before you go home tonight, I need to talk to you."

Lucie nodded her head but didn't ask him to elaborate, and for that Kane was grateful. No matter what, he knew she was going to argue with him and probably be a little pissed off that Kane had already arranged for her to be off work for an entire week, but at this point, he didn't give a shit.

The other night had been a precursor to what Kane wanted from her. Now he just needed to seal the deal.

AT THREE O'CLOCK, Lucie was dead on her feet. The bar had cleared out at two, when the decision-maker lights had come on, yet the McCoy crowd had stuck around for longer than she'd expected. Something about a celebration, although Lucie hadn't understood what they were celebrating. Nor did she ask.

As she walked past the bar, half tempted to sneak out without talking to Kane, she found herself stopping abruptly. The scene she was witnessing caused something dark and bitter to flood her system.

There, at the other end of the bar, was Kane ... and some blonde floozy who seemed to be cozying up to him quite nicely. To his credit, it didn't appear Kane was at all interested in the overly intoxicated woman, but there was a jolt of possessiveness that flooded through her, making her want to scratch the woman's eyes out.

Never having been the catty type, Lucie smiled in spite of herself. After the night Kane had stayed at her apartment, something had undoubtedly changed between the two of them, yet they hadn't spoken much since. He'd visited Haley just like normal each day, but they still had yet to have the conversation that was looming over both of them.

Feeling a little bold, and a lot possessive, Lucie approached Kane and the woman just to see what was going on.

"Let me call you a cab," Kane told the blonde, turning back to the bar.

"I'd much prefer you to take me home," the woman said, although the words were jumbled together and slurred. When the woman grabbed his arm, effectively stopping his efforts to reach the phone, Lucie interjected.

"I'll call for you," Lucie offered, glaring at the woman and not looking at Kane.

"Thanks, baby." Kane's words penetrated her brain, and Lucie froze in place, a strange but not uncomfortable tingle just beneath her skin.

Did he have any idea what he'd just said? A bright ember of hope bloomed in Lucie's chest, and a smile graced her lips. Reaching for the phone, she quickly dialed the cab company's number that was taped just beneath the bar.

A minute later, she turned back to the woman, who was still hanging on Kane, although he looked more than a little irritated at this point. When their eyes met, there was a plea for help in the turbulent gray orbs, and Lucie almost smiled. Almost. It was comical to see the big, bad, surly Kane Steele needing help to fend off a poor, helpless drunk woman.

Instead of ignoring him, like she would do normally, Lucie moved closer. "Cab will be here in five."

"Thank you," Kane mouthed, his eyes glued to her lips, which made Lucie's thighs quiver. She subconsciously licked her lips, and to her surprise, Kane groaned.

"You're killing me, baby."

Lucie had never considered herself the kind of woman that a man would want with the type of desire she saw in Kane's eyes. But she'd seen it before from him, and quite frankly, it empowered her.

Over the last few years, Lucie had lost touch with herself, focusing more on being Haley's mom and nothing more. She worked, she slept, she took care of her precious little girl, but beyond that, she'd become a shell of the woman she had once been.

She'd become the meek, timid woman she hated, but when Kane looked at her like that, she felt her old self deep down, begging to get out. Interestingly enough, she reflected back on the night he had come to her apartment and all but insisted she go down on him in her shower, and her body flared to life once more.

Not that Lucie had ever been the flirty type, but she had been fairly popular with both men and women. She knew what she looked like, knew that men hit on her every single night at the bar, but she figured that was primarily the booze talking. Except in high school, she had been sought after by the boys, but she'd been the nerdy type, so she'd spent four years ignoring them in hopes of making something of her life.

That hadn't happened, though, but not because she hadn't tried. The turn of events in her life had sent her down a different path than she'd originally planned, and Lucie had found herself taking care of her mother for a few years right after high school. Thankfully, they had found some truly excellent doctors, who'd managed to get her mother back on her feet, after four successful back surgeries to repair her spine after a horrible car accident had all but paralyzed her. It had been a long recovery, but her mother was a different woman today than she had been back then.

However, it had come at Lucie's expense, though she would never admit it to her mother. Instead, once her mother was back on her feet, Lucie had come to work at Club Destiny, hoping to make enough money to save for college.

Then another turn of events — namely Kane — had altered her course yet again, and here she was standing before him, almost six years later still employed as a bartender slash waitress and doing everything to raise her beautiful little girl, who'd been her miracle in a particularly dark time. And still, she had let the dark cloud of her life take over. Until recently. Until that night when Kane had finally come to her, finally insisted that they give in to whatever was still brewing between them. And now she felt like a different person.

Feeling even more brazen than before, Lucie approached Kane. Placing her hand on his chest, she successfully inserted herself between him and the floozy, who was barely balancing on those four-inch heels. Letting her eyes skim his mouth briefly, Lucie then met his gaze and smiled. "Let me walk her out and then we can talk."

It was Kane's turn to nod, not saying a word, but she could see the heat reflected in his eyes.

"Come on, honey," Lucie told the woman, gently touching her arm. "The cab should be here now."

As Lucie walked the woman out, she managed to get her address so she could tell the taxi driver where to take her. After a somewhat teary good-bye on the other woman's part, the way-too-intoxicated woman flopped into the cab and was on her way. That's why Lucie didn't drink anymore. That and what had happened between her and Kane that one night so many years ago.

Once back inside, Lucie ventured over to the bar, watching Kane as he quickly ran through a list of items in front of him before their eyes met again.

"Thanks," he said as she approached.

She could only smile. "I really need to get home. I promise I'll call when I get there."

"I want to take you and Haley somewhere," Kane blurted, and Lucie had to think hard to process what he was saying.

"It's the middle of the night," she replied, figuring he already realized that, but she had to state the obvious anyway.

Then he laughed, and the dark, rich sound of it rumbled through her, making her want things she'd never thought she'd want again.

"I wasn't talking about tonight," he clarified, grinning from ear to ear.

"Oh." She knew that.

"Tomorrow," he stated, taking a step closer and putting one hand on her hip.

Lucie glanced around nervously, making sure no one saw them. She clearly didn't have any problem with Kane touching her, but she certainly wasn't interested in letting the other employees see them.

"Where are we going?" she inquired. She was tired, her feet hurt, and she was sure Haley would be up early, but Lucie wouldn't deny wanting to see Kane.

"Hawaii," he said, his eyes locked with hers.

Lucie expected to see humor on his face, so what she saw surprised her. He was serious.

"I can't miss work, Kane. You know that," she told him.

Although he was paying child support now, Lucie was still trying to make ends meet. She was saving up money so that she could move her and Haley to another apartment in another part of town before her daughter started kindergarten. The area they were in wasn't safe, and Lucie was eager to start over somewhere else. Soon.

"Your time off has already been approved. With pay," Kane stated, and Lucie jerked away from him.

"*What?*" How could he? Had he actually asked Luke to give her time off with pay?

"I told Luke that we both needed a week off," he replied, putting his hands in his pockets.

"How dare you?" she asked. Lucie wasn't sure why she was so angry, but she was. Kane didn't have any right to do such a thing. If she wanted time off, it was her responsibility to ask for it. Not his.

"I want to spend time with you and Haley," Kane said, his voice lowered, tilting his head in that way that made Lucie's defenses go down.

Not this time. "Go fuck yourself, Kane," she yelled, and without another thought or another word, she turned and walked out.

# Chapter *Six*

KANE POUNDED ON the door for the second time. Initially, he'd tried for soft, but Lucie obviously wasn't going to answer. Considering it was closing in on three thirty in the morning, he knew one of her neighbors was probably going to call the police on him any minute now.

"Open the door, Lucie," he demanded, keeping his voice low.

When he heard the lock disengage, he breathed a sigh of relief. The woman was stubborn as hell.

"Would you keep your voice down?" Lucie barked as she pulled the door open. "Haley's asleep."

Staring down at her, Kane fought to keep his smile to himself. He liked the way she looked when she was pissed. Maybe that was a little masochistic on his part, but seeing Lucie all fired up stirred his blood.

Not waiting for an invite, Kane moved inside the apartment before shutting and locking the door behind him. Lucie was already in the kitchen by the time he caught up with her. Without haste, Kane grabbed her arm, backed her against the refrigerator, and pinned her mouth with his lips. Her initial reaction was to try to fight him off, but that didn't last but a second before he found himself being pulled into her.

Kane groaned, devouring her sweet taste as she scored his scalp with her fingernails, biting his lip with her sharp little teeth as she began rubbing up against him like a cat. The woman was smoldering, and he needed her. Right there.

"Let's move this to the bedroom," he stated when he pulled back, cupping her head with both hands. She looked up at him dazed and confused, and he smiled. "I'm going to be inside of you in less than two minutes," he warned, "and I don't think you want our daughter walking in to see that."

When it looked like Lucie might argue with him, Kane kissed her again, turning her so that he could back her down the short hall. As soon as they entered her bedroom, he tapped the door shut with his foot and began unbuttoning her shirt.

When her mouth moved to his neck, Kane growled, loving the way she nipped his skin, chasing the sting with her tongue as he tried to unhook the buttons with his hands trapped between them.

"Fuck." The curse left his lips when she pulled his shirt open without bothering to unbutton it, the sound of buttons pinging against the walls all around them.

It was probably a record, he thought to himself as he pulled Lucie down on top of him onto her bed. Somehow they'd managed to remove all of their clothes without ever breaking contact. The feel of her skin against his had Kane sighing. She was soft to his hard, and he loved the feel of her skin beneath his hands. Aside from Haley's smooth, baby-like skin, Lucie was the softest thing he'd ever touched.

"Ride me, Lucie," Kane demanded, gripping her hips and moving her so that their bodies aligned the way he needed them to. "Sit on my cock, baby. Right fucking now."

He didn't give a damn if he sounded crass. He just needed to be buried inside of this woman. Now.

Kane could see the innocent look in her eyes, and he realized she was nervous. Damn, the woman could turn him on like no one else. He liked her fiery defiance, but he loved this innocence just as much.

"Lift up," he encouraged her, gripping his cock in his hand and penetrating her entrance gently. "Take me inside of you, Lucie."

Kane groaned as her body engulfed him, but his mouth was covered with her hand, and he met her eyes. She was trying to smile, but he knew what she felt, because he was feeling it too. She was so damn tight, her pussy clenching him as she eased down on his shaft.

Pulling her chest flush against his, Kane gripped her hips and thrust up into her in one swift movement that had her crying out. "Kiss me, dammit," he grumbled from beneath her hand.

Lucie replaced her hand with her mouth, and the invasion of her tongue was so welcome Kane had to hold still for a moment for fear that he might just lose control. He could feel it in his chest. There was a tingling that started somewhere in the center of his body, but it wasn't his release. This was something different. Something unexpected but so incredible he wasn't sure he ever wanted to come down from this high.

Wrapping one arm around her head and placing his other hand against the small of her back, Kane held her against him, trying to keep her from moving. When she began rocking her hips and moaning into his mouth, he knew he wasn't going to last long enough to make this good for her if she kept this up.

Letting her go, he pushed her shoulders until she was sitting on him again, and he linked their hands together, holding his arms up so that she could use him as leverage.

"Fuck me, Lucie." He ground out the words, clenching his teeth as her pussy clenched around his dick.

Obviously unfamiliar with the position, Lucie began doing as he instructed, and although the feeling was exquisite, Kane needed to control her movements. In a blur of motion, he flipped her onto her back, never pulling out of her body. Once he was on top of her, he began thrusting his hips hard and fast against hers, burying his cock deeper into her body as she closed her eyes and threw her head back.

"Open them," he growled. "Open your eyes and watch me, Lucie." He had no idea why it was so important that he maintain eye contact with her, but Kane felt it was critical. Their bodies were speaking in ways that words never could, but the connection was far deeper than that, and he wanted to see into her soul.

"God, yes, baby," he groaned, slowing his pace as he slipped one hand between them, finding her clit with his fingers. "You feel so damn good."

As he began strumming her clit gently, Lucie's moans intensified until she was clawing his shoulders, her hips bucking up off of the mattress.

"Are you going to come for me?" he asked, sinking deeper and deeper into her with every thrust, increasing the pressure of his finger against her clit with every jarring movement. "Tell me, Lucie. Tell me when you come."

Kane barely managed to control himself, continuing to pound harder, faster, until he was sweating and shaking with the strength of his release as it rushed upon him without warning. Slamming into her once, twice, three times, Kane felt the way her inner muscles squeezed his cock, almost painfully tight as Lucie moaned into the darkened room, her sharp little nails digging into his skin as she stilled.

As she came apart beneath him, Kane followed her over into the glorious abyss.

THERE WAS SOMETHING to be said about angry sex, Lucie thought to herself as she lay against Kane, her head propped on his chest as his heartbeat thumped slowly in her ear. He was so warm, so strong as he held her close, his finger drawing circles up and down her spine.

It was still dark outside, but Lucie knew that was only going to last a little while longer. Dawn wasn't far off, and despite the fact that she wanted him there more than she wanted anything else, Lucie knew it wouldn't be appropriate for Haley to find him in her bed. They probably had another hour at best before her early riser was up and at it.

"Why didn't you tell me?" Kane asked, his gravelly voice penetrating the darkness.

Lucie's body stiffened. The question was a long time coming, but for some reason, she hadn't expected to hear it from him now. Not like this. She knew this wasn't going to be an easy conversation for them to have, and if nothing else, he was going to be angry with her. All over again.

When she tried to pull away, Kane stopped her by firmly pressing his arm against her back.

"Don't leave me," he warned, keeping her pinned in place by his heavy arm. "Talk to me. Don't pull away from me, Lucie."

Laying her head back against his chest, Lucie inhaled deeply as she tried to gather her thoughts. When it came to her reasons for not telling Kane he was a father, she knew they probably wouldn't sound as reasonable once she stated them out loud.

Honestly, she hadn't meant to hurt anyone, although that's exactly what had happened. Both Haley and Kane had suffered from her decision, and there were many nights she had lain in bed wishing she could change how she'd handled the situation. Figuring he deserved to know everything, Lucie started at the beginning.

"I found out I was pregnant when I was three and a half months along," she began. "I hadn't felt well for a couple of months, but I figured it was my emotions playing havoc on me."

"Why?" Kane asked, brushing her hair with his fingertips.

Lucie knew her confession was probably going to push Kane away, but she decided to go for it anyway. "After you and I slept together, my feelings for you only intensified," she stated and then paused to see if he would react. When he didn't, she continued, "I think I had been attracted to you all along, but I knew better because you were — are — my boss."

That was the hardest part of everything. Kane was still her boss.

"The night I drove you home, I had originally done so with good intentions. I didn't want you to drive drunk," she admitted, although she had already told him this part. She had just left off the emotional aspect. "When you invited me in, I knew I should've said no, but part of me just wanted to be closer to you."

To her surprise, Kane pulled her closer against him, and when she felt his lips against her head, she had to choke back the tears that threatened to fall.

"Honestly, had I realized you were so drunk that you wouldn't even remember sleeping with me, I wouldn't have gone inside."

"Tell me what happened."

"I already did." Lucie had shared the high-level details with him already, back when she'd told him he was Haley's father.

"You told me that you drove me home and that we slept together. I want to know all of the details."

Lucie sighed. It wasn't like she couldn't recall every single second of that night, because she had relived it over and over for the past six years.

"Tell me," Kane whispered into the darkness.

With another deep sigh, Lucie began explaining, "You invited me inside, and I agreed. Then you offered me a drink, and I refused, hoping you wouldn't get one, either. I knew you were drunk, but I hadn't realized just how intoxicated you really were."

Lucie closed her eyes, going back to that night...

*"Touch me, baby."* *The insistence in Kane's tone was palpable, and Lucie wanted to give herself over to this man. Even if for just one night, she wanted to know what it felt like to be in his arms, to feel his mouth, his skin, all of him against her.*

*With her palms flat against his chest, Lucie met his gaze, looking up into the swirling gray orbs, trying to decipher what he was thinking. Reading Kane's mind was impossible.*

*"What do you want from me, Lucie?" he asked when she didn't move.*

*"You," she admitted, knowing she was making a decision that she would never be able to undo.*

*"I've waited so long to hear you say that," Kane told her, sliding his fingers into her hair and pulling her head closer.*

*When her lips met his, the world exploded around her. Nothing and everything changed at that moment. The warm, firm press of his lips, the insistent plunge of his tongue into her mouth had Lucie feeling drunk, and she knew she wasn't.*

She could taste the bourbon on his tongue, smell the faint hint of cigarette smoke and beer on his clothes. Kane was kissing her, and as his tongue became more and more insistent, Lucie gave herself over to the feelings she had pushed to the far recesses of her heart for so long.

When Kane pulled back, he cupped her face in his hands, and Lucie stared up at him, waiting for him to tell her what he wanted. As his thumb brushed over her lower lip, Lucie slowly traced the tip with her tongue and reveled in his sharp intake of breath.

"I want to feel your mouth on my cock," he told her, his eyes locked on her mouth. "I want to fuck those sweet lips."

His words sent a warm throb between her thighs. Never would she have thought she would like such vulgar words, but they were so thrilling coming from Kane's mouth. Lucie found she was nodding her head in agreement, and Kane took a step back from her, immediately pulling his belt open before releasing the button and zipper on his slacks and then lowering them over his hips.

His cock, thick and heavy, sprang free, and Lucie closed her eyes for a second. She could do this. She had dreamed about this. Maybe the setting was different, or the circumstances, but it had always been Kane in her dreams.

When he put one hand on her shoulder, the other on her head and pushed her to her knees, Lucie lowered herself willingly, keeping her eyes trained on his throbbing erection.

Kane gripped his cock in one hand, guiding it toward her mouth, and Lucie fought the panic that surged up from somewhere deep inside of her. She wanted him, and this was her chance.

"Open your mouth," Kane growled, and Lucie looked up at him unexpectedly. His tone was aggressive, laced with what sounded like anger mixed with passion, and the desire that she detected in his beautiful gray eyes was intense.

Pain laced her scalp as Kane gripped her hair more forcefully, pushing the swollen head of his cock against her lips until she opened her mouth, taking him inside, trying her best to surround him with her whole mouth.

He was larger than she'd expected, although she wasn't quite sure what she had expected. The grip on her hair was both painful and sensual at the same time. When he began pushing in deeper before retreating, over and over, Lucie instinctively wrapped her lips around him.

She'd never done this before. In fact, Lucie had never been with a man before Kane. Not like this anyway. There had been one man in her past who she had slept with, but that was so long ago she felt like this was the first time. Considering her past experience was with her high school boyfriend, she knew that was nothing compared to being with Kane.

"Suck me," Kane growled, and his tone reflected more of a demand than a request. "Wrap your lips around my dick, Lucie."

She did as he told her, trying to accommodate his size as well as keep up with the forceful way he was thrusting into her mouth. He was more aggressive than she'd expected, but Lucie wanted to please him, so she continued to try and take more of him. When his hands fisted in her hair, holding her perfectly still, Lucie almost panicked.

"Put your hands on my thighs and don't move them," Kane demanded.

Lucie once again did as he instructed, and the instant her hands were on his powerful thighs, Kane gripped her hair even harder and began shoving deeper into her mouth as she tried to keep from gagging.

"That's it, Lucie. Let me fuck that beautiful mouth. Take all of me. Awww, damn, that's good."

Kane's words sounded like encouragement, and Lucie could feel the tension increase in his legs as he pushed harder, deeper, faster. When she felt the broad head of his penis hit the back of her throat, she did panic, but Kane held her still, pulling out of her mouth.

"I need to fuck you, Lucie." His grip in her hair didn't lessen, and she found herself having to rise to her feet to keep from crying out in pain.

"Take off your clothes," he ordered, and Lucie started to do as he said. She hadn't expected it to be like this, but the terse words stirred something deep inside of her. He was turning her on, and she was torn between confusion and desire.

Quickly, she managed to unbutton her slacks, but before she could get them halfway down her legs, Kane was turning her until she was facing the counter, his hand pushing her down until her breasts were crushed against the granite countertop. Without warning, Kane slammed into her from behind, and she cried out as pain crashed through her.

"Lucie." Kane's voice sounded closer to her ear, and for a second, he wasn't the demanding, take-charge man she'd just been introduced to. "Baby, your pussy feels so damn good. I've dreamed about fucking you just like this."

Lucie's body tensed at his words, a desperate hunger filling her as she ached for him to continue. Despite the fact that his demands were making her nervous, her body still wanted him.

The warmth of his body disappeared from her back, his hands gripping her hips painfully tight before he began slamming into her over and over.

Lucie didn't know what was happening to her, but her body tightened, a sharp, sudden tingle erupted deep in her core, and she was moaning his name over and over. Her orgasm slammed into her, making her shake as he continued to fuck her deeper, harder, over and over, until finally, long minutes later, Kane shouted her name as he came deep inside of her.

# Chapter *Seven*

KANE WAS LEANING over Lucie as she stared up at him. The story she'd just told him shattered his soul. To know he had treated her so crudely their very first time made his gut tighten. No wonder she had kept such a monumental secret from him. He was lucky she'd even talked to him again.

"I'm so sorry," he whispered.

Lucie's hands came up to cup his face, and she stunned him with a smile. "It wasn't a bad thing, Kane. And that's not why I didn't tell you."

*It wasn't?*

"I don't understand."

"In my head, it all made sense," she began, running her hand through his hair and sending a chill down his spine. "I wasn't trying to keep Haley from you. I was trying to protect you. I didn't want to burden you, because I knew what happened between us wouldn't have happened if you were sober. It was my fault... And you didn't remember, so—"

Kane cut her off, pressing his fingers against her lips. "Don't say it. It takes two, Lucie, and I was just as much a part of that night as you were. You can't even begin to imagine how many times I wanted to take you just like that," Kane said, closing his eyes briefly. "I would have done it differently, I promise."

He would've never been so rough on her during their first time. He knew he wasn't a gentle lover, and he didn't make excuses for himself, but he would've never put himself first the way he apparently had that night. He could blame it on the alcohol, he knew, but it didn't make a damn bit of difference. He was responsible for his own actions, and what he'd done was inexcusable.

"I never should've kept her from you," Lucie whispered in the dark. "I didn't mean to hurt either one of you."

Kane heard her sob, felt the tear that brushed his finger as it slid down her cheek and into her hair, making his heart seize in his chest. A million times he had imagined how this conversation would go, but never once had he dreamed it would be like this.

"What do you say we start over?" he asked, knowing it wasn't entirely possible because they already had an amazing daughter together, and he wouldn't change that even if he could.

"How?"

"You and Haley go to Hawaii with me. One week, Lucie. Let's spend that one week getting to know each other."

The dim light from the rising sun penetrated the room, and Kane could faintly make out her face. Lucie was looking at him, considering what he was asking of her. Not that he blamed her if she said no, but he hoped and prayed she wouldn't.

"Please," he added before pressing his lips to hers.

"All right," she finally said, long seconds later. "We'll go with you."

Kane would've fist pumped the air, but instead, he chose to kiss her. Hard.

Pulling back, he smiled down on her. "We have to be at the airport by eight."

Kane moved toward the gate, carrying Haley in one arm and her car seat in the other while Lucie trailed behind them pulling one of her carry-on suitcases that contained things for Haley. They nearly had to sprint to their gate, and for once, Kane didn't mind that he was running behind.

Normally he would've been pissed and stressed at the fact that he was risking missing his plane, but due to the circumstances, he could only smile. Apparently, it took a lot longer to pack a child and her mother for a week-long trip than it did to pack for himself.

The instant he'd told Lucie what time their flight left, she had practically tossed him out of bed and onto the floor. Obviously she needed more than just an hour notice, so he had given her two, and here they were, almost running through the terminal. Since they were in first class, Kane wasn't all that worried about whether they were at the gate thirty minutes before the flight left, but now they only had about fifteen minutes to spare, so he was forcing Lucie to keep up.

By the time they were seated, Haley busy with her coloring book and crayons, Lucie looked a little frazzled.

"You okay?" Kane asked, sliding his hand into hers. Since Haley had insisted on sitting by the window, Kane was lucky to have Lucie beside him.

"I will be," she muttered, thrusting her hand through her hair and glancing over at him sideways.

"What's wrong?" She was obviously not doing nearly as well as she was pretending.

"I hate flying," she admitted, looking straight ahead at the seat in front of her.

Kane turned to face Lucie, tipping her chin so that she looked at him. "It'll be okay," he whispered, not wanting Haley to hear him. "Thank you."

"For what?" she laughed, sounding almost hysterical.

Kane gripped her fingers tightly, pulling her hand into his lap. "For coming with me."

After what Lucie had told him earlier that morning, Kane considered himself lucky that she even gave him the time of day. Knowing what she had gone through the very first time they were together, he had vowed to make it all up to her, and he was starting with this trip. It was time for him to show Lucie just how special she was to him.

LUCIE DIDN'T LIKE flying. That wasn't a secret. However, she'd honestly expected Haley to be the one on the verge of tears, not her. But, for her little girl's sake, Lucie was sucking it up, being strong. There was nothing to worry about, she knew. Statistics showed that there was a greater chance of being in a car wreck than in a plane crash.

She hated statistics. They didn't help to alleviate any of her tension, so she didn't know why she even bothered to recite them.

Holding Kane's hand, attempting to absorb his strength, she tried to divert her thoughts to something more productive. Ever since she'd agreed to go to Hawaii with him, she'd been in a rush. Considering she'd had no idea how quickly she had to get ready, it was a good thing he'd finally told her when he had. Somehow, she still wasn't sure how, they had made it to their plane on time.

The captain's voice came over the intercom, and Lucie damn near came out of her chair. When Kane pulled her hand back into his lap, his thumb gently sweeping back and forth over her palm, she managed to relax. Slightly.

Fifteen minutes later, they were in the air without a single hiccup in the takeoff. Too bad they still had to do this one more time. Kane hadn't mentioned it until they were signing in at the airline counter, but they had to change planes in Los Angeles and do this all over again. Her stomach was queasy just thinking about it.

"Mommy," Haley said, grabbing the sleeve of her T-shirt and pulling gently. "Can I watch a movie?"

"Of course, honey," Lucie replied, grateful for something to do.

Sitting still for several hours was going to be a difficult task for her, and likely impossible for Haley, but she was hoping they could get through it. At that point, they'd get to spend five glorious days in Maui, and Lucie was secretly looking forward to some relaxing time on the beach. After what had happened this morning between her and Kane, she needed a little time to absorb everything anyway.

Telling him the events of the first night they were together had been easier than she'd anticipated, but seeing his own reaction to it had been harder. She'd been with Kane twice now in the last few days, and she detected that strong, alpha presence and the hunger that he barely managed to contain. Considering what they had gone through that very first time, she'd expected it. What she hadn't expected was the guilt in his eyes when he looked at her. He hadn't hurt her. Not by a long shot. Yet looking into those intense gray eyes, she wouldn't have known that. As much as she tried to reassure him, she knew Kane wasn't going easy on himself. What could she say? "Please, I like it rough"? No, that probably wouldn't go over terribly well, even if it were the truth.

She only hoped that he didn't withdraw from her now that she had told him. Lucie was all for making love, the mating of souls and all that, but there were times when down and dirty was the only way to go. In fact, she craved that from Kane. For the last few years, she'd imagined so many scenarios, each of them leaving her hot and bothered and in desperate need of release that never seemed to come.

Now... Well, now she had the opportunity to experience everything she'd ever dreamed of. As long as Kane didn't go all perfect gentleman on her.

# Chapter *Eight*

KANE WAS SO proud of his girls. Yes, that's what he had been considering them for the past twelve hours during the flights and a layover in L.A. Both Haley and Lucie had done tremendously well for such a long trip, but now as they entered the posh condominium facing the beach, he was grateful they would have five full days of relaxation.

Or he hoped they would.

Apparently, Haley had gotten her second wind somewhere between the airport and the condo, and keeping up with her was becoming increasingly more difficult. She was also getting a little cranky, but Kane couldn't necessarily blame her.

"Let's order room service and watch a movie," Kane offered and watched his daughter's eyes light up.

"Can we, Mommy?" she asked, turning to face Lucie.

Lucie glanced over at Kane and smiled.

"Of course we can."

"Can I pick out what we're going to eat, Daddy?"

Kane had been walking across the room, and he stopped mid-stride, his legs no longer working the way they were supposed to. Turning to face the most beautiful little girl in the entire world, he didn't know whether he should laugh or cry. Had she just called him Daddy? He still wondered whether his ears were betraying him.

He had dreamed of the day she would start calling him Daddy, but he'd known he would never force her to. Hearing her call him Kane had been harder on him than he'd thought it would be, but now, his heart was doing somersaults in his chest, and he was scared he actually might literally cry.

He looked up, met Lucie's eyes, and saw that she was crying. One single tear rolled silently down her cheek, and she smiled so sweetly at him.

"Of course you can, honey," he answered Haley as he turned back toward the dresser he had been taking his clothes to. He needed a minute.

Or maybe twenty.

He admitted to feeling an overwhelming resentment when Lucie had finally informed him that he was Haley's father. Despite the fact that he'd insisted on a paternity test, he had believed her. Aside from the anger, he'd felt something else, too. Paralyzing joy. No matter what, he would never get the time back that he had missed with Haley, but Kane had never thought he'd have children, so finding out the incredibly beautiful little girl was his had shifted something deep down inside of him.

"Are you okay?" Lucie's voice was soft, her hand warm on his back as she came to stand beside him.

"I will be." He would be better than okay, that was for damn sure. He just needed some time to catch his breath.

"She loves you," Lucie stated, sounding as though she was trying to make him feel better. What she didn't know was that there was no way he would ever feel better than he did right at that moment. For Haley to accept him as her father, even if she didn't quite know what that meant, made everything better.

Pushing the drawer in, Kane took a deep breath and then turned to face his daughter. Walking quickly over to her, he scooped her up in his arms, turned her over his shoulder before flipping her back onto her feet while she belted out that sweet little-girl giggle.

"All right, kiddo. What're we gonna have for dinner?"

LUCIE SAT CROSS-LEGGED on the bed beside Haley, Kane on the opposite side of the bed leaning back against the headboard with a plate balanced on his flat stomach. They had rented a movie, one of Haley's favorites, and the two of them were waiting patiently for her to fall asleep. She was fighting it, every step of the way.

After Kane had ordered food, they'd finished unpacking and set up Haley's things in the second bedroom. Lucie still wasn't sure how the sleeping arrangements were going to work, because sleeping in the same bed with Kane was what she wanted more than anything, but she didn't want Haley to get any mixed messages, either.

They weren't a couple. In fact, Lucie wasn't even sure what they were. They were on vacation, and yes, if she had anything to say about it, she and Kane would enjoy a little horizontal time together, but she knew once they were back in the real world, nothing would have changed. She wasn't sure she honestly wanted it to, either.

Kane and Haley were obviously making progress with their relationship, and she had to give credit to Kane. He had asked her permission to seek counseling for him and Haley in order to try and work through some of the changes that were inevitable in the little girl's life. Apparently, Haley was adapting better than any of them had expected her to.

She'd called Kane Daddy, and Lucie's heart had undoubtedly missed a beat, or maybe two. Watching while Kane absorbed the words had been one of the most heart-wrenching things she had ever seen. At first, she'd thought he might cry, but the big tough guy had managed to get through the moment without even a hint of a tear. He was stronger than she was.

Since that moment, Haley had probably called him Daddy no less than fifty times, and he seemed to eat it up every single time. Lucie couldn't blame him. This was a huge milestone for the two of them, and she was just happy she had the opportunity to witness it for herself. After all the heartache she had caused, seeing the bond between father and daughter grow stronger every day didn't make her guilt lessen any, but she was grateful for the choice she finally had made.

"She's asleep," Kane whispered, breaking Lucie from her thoughts. Glancing over, she noticed that Haley was, in fact, asleep, propped on Kane's shoulder, her teddy bear tucked beneath her arm. Glancing over at the television, she noticed the closing credits were rolling down the screen.

Damn, she had missed most of the movie thanks to her wandering thoughts.

Lucie climbed out of the bed and started to reach for Haley, but Kane waved her off easily. "I'll carry her if you want to pull the blankets back on her bed."

Making quick work of getting the bed ready for Haley, Lucie watched while Kane tucked her in before standing back and staring down at her.

"She's beautiful," Kane whispered. Lucie barely heard the words, but she felt the sentiment. He was a proud father, and that made Lucie's heart break even more. How could she have been so stupid for so long?

Turning quickly, she escaped back into the other bedroom and quickly grabbed the empty plates and a bowl of popcorn Haley had been munching on earlier. With hurried movements, she returned everything to the small kitchen, rinsed the plates before stacking them in the dish drainer and dumping the popcorn in the trash can.

When Lucie was finished, she returned to the living area, studying the couch to see whether it folded out to a bed as she assumed. She knew there was an extra blanket and pillow in the hall closet, and this would work perfectly, even if it didn't fold out.

"Are you okay?" Kane's voice startled her, and she jumped, turning to face him. Surprised to see him just a couple of inches behind her, Lucie nearly stumbled backward, and she would have if he hadn't slipped his arms around her and stopped her.

"I'm fine." Okay, so she didn't even sound fine to her own ears.

"You don't look fine." Kane smiled. "Well, that's not entirely true. You look fucking hot, but you don't look happy."

Despite herself, Lucie smiled. Kane had a way of doing that to her.

"I was just trying to figure out how this makes into a bed," she explained, her hand flailing backward, hinting at the sofa behind her.

"Well, I've got a better idea." Kane lifted her easily, and Lucie was forced to wrap her legs around him.

"I don't want Haley to see us in bed together," she murmured against his neck, giving in to the emotions that were overwhelming her.

Kane stopped, leaning his head back slightly so she was forced to look up at him.

"Do you trust me, Luce?" he asked, and she was instantly mesmerized by his smoky gray gaze.

"I do," she said honestly. Lucie had always trusted him. That had never been her issue. The reason she'd kept Haley a secret from him hadn't been because she didn't trust him with their daughter. She had done the unthinkable because she'd been trying to protect him. In her mind, she hadn't wanted Kane to feel trapped.

"Then do exactly what I tell you to do," he whispered as he continued moving toward the bedroom.

Kane carried her to the bed and then stood her back on her feet. Once she was planted firmly on the ground, she looked up at him, noticing the passion and anticipation that had replaced the concern she'd detected a few seconds ago.

"I'll be right back. When I get back, I want you naked." Kane kept his gaze leveled on hers. "And I want you standing right here where I left you."

Lucie nodded her head in understanding, although she felt a little out of sorts. This was new to her. This place. This man. This feeling. All of it churned together, making it difficult to breathe, much less think.

Kane turned and disappeared from the room. For two, maybe three seconds, Lucie hesitated. Finally, when the warmth that had started in her tummy penetrated her limbs, she began to move, quickly disrobing, tossing her clothes on the chair in the corner.

When Kane returned, Lucie was stunned silent as he stalked toward her sans his shirt. The man's body was drool worthy. The way his shoulders bunched, his biceps flexed, and the perfectly sculpted triangle of his tricep tightened had her clenching her thighs together. That was only part of it. The ripple effect of his washboard abs made her want to drop to her knees and trace every luscious line with her tongue until she'd gotten her fill of him.

Lucie was pretty sure that would never happen, and she got the impression Kane knew it.

# Chapter *Nine*

LOOKING AT LUCIE had never been a hardship. In fact, looking at her was one of the highlights of his day. That's when they were at work. But here, right now, seeing her naked and waiting for him, Kane wasn't sure he'd ever seen anyone as beautiful as her. Dressed, Lucie was stunning, no matter what she wore. Naked, she was captivating.

Kane shut the door behind him, flipping the lock to avoid any mishaps in the event Haley woke up in the next hour or so. An hour didn't seem like nearly enough time to do what he wanted to do with Lucie, but he also wasn't sure he could last more than a few minutes. The woman made his skin overheat and his dick react like a hair trigger.

"I think you're a little overdressed," she stated in that sweet, raspy tone that sent chills down his spine. He loved her seductive husky voice and watching her heart-shaped lips form every syllable.

"You think?" Kane knew he was overdressed, and the only thing he was wearing was his jeans. He'd disposed of his shoes and socks before the three of them had taken their spots in the big bed to watch a movie. After checking on Haley and making sure the main door was locked, he'd dropped his shirt somewhere along the way.

"I want to taste you." Lucie's words surprised him, and based on the way her eyes widened, he was pretty sure she hadn't intended to speak them out loud.

His only response was the animalistic growl that surged from somewhere deep in his chest. As he closed the gap between them, Kane pulled the button on his jeans from the mooring and then slid the zipper down. Once he was within touching distance of her, he stopped, staring down into her chocolate-brown eyes and feeling as though someone had sucker-punched him. She made him breathless, and the anticipation he felt at the thought of touching her again made him feel like a teenager.

Kane had been with a number of women in his lifetime and experienced more than his fair share of raunchy, take-what-you-want sex, but none of that compared to even the buildup he felt when he was with Lucie.

His mind drifted back to the conversation they had shared just that morning, and he almost flinched at the memory of what she'd said he had done to her. Although her description had never hinted at her distaste for what had happened between them, Kane was still mortified at how he had treated her. He was almost grateful that he didn't remember, because he wasn't sure he'd be able to look her in the eyes ever again.

She deserved gentle, loving caresses, not slammed-up-against-the-counter fucking, although that part of him was clawing to get free, to take her without hesitance ... to own her.

"I don't want sweet and gentle," Lucie whispered in the otherwise silent room, her words bringing him back to the moment. For half a second, he had to wonder whether she had read his mind.

"You deserve that," he replied, moving his hands to the gentle curve of her waist, his gaze roaming down the sexy, sleek column of her neck to her collarbone, then beyond. Her breasts were tipped with sweet, dusky pink nipples, hardened and begging for his mouth.

"I want you, Kane," Lucie whispered, taking another step closer until her breasts brushed against his chest. "I don't want gentle right now. I know that's not who you are, and for at least the next few days, while it lasts, I want the real you."

Kane didn't bother to tell Lucie that he was looking for more than the next few days. He had come to terms with that somewhere in the last few months, and last night had solidified it in his mind. He didn't just care about Lucie and her well-being because she was the mother of his child. He loved her. Deeply and with everything he was.

It wasn't something he'd expected to happen, but he wasn't going to fight it, either. There was no point. For most of his life, Kane had wondered whether he would ever have that something more that others had found, and he had all but given up hope. That was until he'd met Lucie.

Not that he could say as much out loud.

"Are you sure?" he asked, although he could see the desire in her warm, dark brown eyes staring up at him.

"Positive," she confirmed, then lifted her hand to his head, sliding her fingers into his hair and pulling him closer until his mouth met hers.

The kiss started out sweet, but within seconds, it took a carnal turn. When Lucie nipped his bottom lip, her fingers lacing into his hair, sending shards of pleasure-pain racing through his scalp, Kane knew this night would be unlike any other.

Pulling back, Kane didn't take his eyes off of her. If she wanted this, he was more than willing to give her everything he kept bottled inside, but he was going to do this his way. It was the only way he knew.

Stepping away for a moment, Kane managed to turn off the lights and pull open the curtains on the oversized sliding glass door in the room. He pulled open the glass, allowing the warm breeze to blow in off of the ocean while the moonlight eased in and provided a romantic glow.

Walking back to Lucie, he took her hand in his, then led her back to the balcony that overlooked the dark waters lapping at the shoreline. It was late, but not too late that there weren't still people outside. He could hear the sounds of a nightclub just around the corner as well as other guests in the adjacent condos.

"What are you doing?" Lucie questioned, sounding a little unsure.

Pressing his mouth to her ear, he whispered, "Shhh. You don't want anyone to hear you, do you?"

Lucie shook her head from side to side, but she didn't move.

"Put your hands on the railing," Kane instructed, keeping his voice low and steady as he stood behind her. "You see those people down there?"

Lucie nodded her head as she wrapped her fingers around the top rail. There wasn't anything between them and the people below on the beach except for a few wrought iron rails and about forty feet of air. With the way the moon shone down on them, Kane knew if anyone were to look up, they'd get a more remarkable view than the one from where he stood. The moon sitting low on the ocean was nothing in comparison to Lucie and her elegant beauty.

"If you make a sound, they'll hear you," he told her, sliding his hands down the strong curve of her back and then over the luscious swells of her butt before cupping each globe in his hands. "And if they hear you, they'll look up here. Do you want them to watch you?"

Lucie didn't immediately answer him. She stood stone still, her fingers still wrapped around the metal bar, her back straight, and her chest heaving from the labored breaths she took.

On each side of them was a solid wall that blocked them from any prying eyes of their neighbors, but there was nothing in front of them to hide what they were doing. Or about to do.

They were only on the second floor of the beachfront condo, so they weren't that far up off the ground, but with the way the moonlight angled in, they were shrouded in shadows, but not entirely hidden from view. Kane didn't mind anyone watching, in fact, this was one of the more modest places he'd engaged in this type of activity. Not that he'd tell Lucie that.

She'd said she wanted what he could give her. Now, she was going to get a taste of what that meant.

LUCIE COULDN'T BELIEVE she was standing stark naked just a few yards away from a handful of people still hanging out on the beach. They were sitting around a bonfire, so she was pretty sure they weren't paying any attention to what was going on behind them, but she knew if they turned even slightly, they'd see her. Surprisingly, she didn't have the desire to run and hide.

In fact, this was the most erotic thing she'd ever done, and the warmth pooling between her legs was proof of how much she was affected. She hadn't quite known what she was asking for when she'd told Kane that she wanted to experience the real him. For some reason, she hadn't imagined this. However, now that she was standing here, his big, warm hands cupping her butt, she was anticipating so much more.

"Remember, don't take your hands off of the rail. And don't make a sound, or you'll have an audience."

His words were a warning, and they sent a tingle of excitement racing through her bloodstream.

When his hands moved farther south, sliding between her thighs, Lucie whimpered but immediately bit her bottom lip in order to stay quiet.

"Spread your legs wider," Kane directed, his voice low and laced with a hunger she practically could feel.

Sliding her feet farther apart, Lucie continued to watch the people down below them, wondering whether anyone had noticed what they were doing.

Kane's warmth disappeared from behind her for a moment, but then he returned, and she felt something soft fall to the ground. Glancing down between her legs, she noticed one of the pillows from the bed. When he knelt behind her, Lucie could only see his knees and his hard, firm thighs, but she could feel his hands on her bottom again, and another chill ran its course through her. She didn't know what he intended to do, and quite frankly, she didn't honestly care as long as he did something soon.

He placed his hands firmly on her hips, pulling her backward until she was forced to move her feet or fall over. Taking two steps back, she was now leaning closer to the railing, her hands gripping the cool metal bar for all she was worth, her breasts now pointing toward the concrete below her.

Kane's hands once again slid slowly down her hips until they were at the tops of her thighs, and he pushed her legs wider, his hands forcing her butt cheeks apart. Oh! The first brush of his mouth against the delicate tissue of her anus had her flinching. She'd never...

If she hadn't been leaning forward, her head would have fallen back on her shoulders as her body was assaulted with a strange, intensely erotic feeling as his tongue slid down the crease of her ass, momentarily circling her anus before venturing lower, until he was teasing the delicate folds of her pussy with his tongue.

She sucked in a harsh breath, trying not to make a sound as the pleasure ricocheted through her, making her legs tremble. He continued to torment her with his tongue, gliding up and then back down, piercing her anus with his tongue over and over until she wondered whether she would be able to remain standing. Crying out wasn't an option, because she didn't want these people to look up and see what she was doing, but it took every ounce of control she had just to remain quiet.

It was so good. So foreign, yet exciting at the same time. Never in her life had she even imagined a man touching her like that. Never had she thought she would like it as much as she did, either.

A moan escaped her as Kane slid his tongue over her clit, angling his head so that he could place suckling kisses to the throbbing bundle of nerves. The man knew how to use his mouth. There was no way she could stop the onslaught that was barreling forward, threatening to take her knees out with the ecstasy racing through her limbs.

Suddenly, Kane stopped, and Lucie wanted to scream. She was so close! What was he doing?

"Turn around." Kane's deep voice resonated through the night, and Lucie glanced around to ensure no one else heard him before turning to face him where he continued to kneel on the ground at her feet.

"Such a pretty pussy." Kane growled the words, and Lucie leaned against the railing, still holding the top bar with her hands as he positioned her so that her legs were spread once more. From this angle, she could see him, and she watched in silent fascination as he used his large fingers to separate the folds of her pussy before leaning forward and once again stealing her breath with the wicked flick of his tongue.

When his eyes met hers, Lucie choked back a cry, trying to thrust her hips forward in order to increase the friction of his mouth on her clit. He was torturing her. On purpose. The devilish smirk on his face told her he was pushing her. Kane was trying to make her cry out from the overwhelming pleasure, and she feared that if he kept it up, he would get his way.

"Kane," she whispered, trying to keep her voice low so as not to alert those around her to what was happening, but Lucie had a damn hard time holding back.

She was unable to hold back the moan that escaped as he suckled her clit harder, using his tongue to apply just the right amount of pressure to have her ... shattering.

"Oh my...!"

There was no way that she hadn't been heard that time, but Lucie no longer cared as her body splintered into a million pieces, right there on the balcony for everyone to see and hear.

# Chapter *Ten*

KANE STOOD TO his full height, pulling Lucie against him as her body trembled from her orgasm. He couldn't help but smile as he held her close. After lifting her into his arms, he carried her back inside, heaving the sliding glass door closed. That was all the show their neighbors would be getting tonight. The rest was just for him.

By the time they reached the bed, Lucie was pulling away from him, and the mischievous smirk told him she was coming up with a devious plan. "What?"

"You know that little saying ... turnabout is fair play?" she asked, a gleam in her chocolate-brown eyes.

He nodded, pulling her up against him once more, cupping her ass with his hands and grinding his steel-hard erection against her core.

"I'm thinking you should have to stand outside while I use my mouth on you," she whispered, her eyes fluttering closed as he continued to grind against her, making sure to rub his cock over her clit.

"Baby, we can go down to the beach for all I care. I've got no shame. I'll let you suck my cock anytime you want." It was no less than the truth. Kane didn't care who watched.

The understanding in her eyes made him smile. He liked that she didn't seem turned off by the idea. As far as Kane was concerned, there'd be plenty more public encounters like that in their future. But for now, he needed to be inside of her.

Wrapping her long hair around his fist, Kane pulled her head back so he could look down into her eyes. "Did you like what I did to you?"

Lucie nodded, but he knew she needed a little more clarification of what exactly he meant.

"Did you enjoy feeling my tongue in your ass?"

Her innocent gaze turned molten as she sucked her bottom lip into her mouth.

"Tell me, Lucie. Did you like when I played with your ass?"

"Yes," she whispered, her body reacting as she began rocking her hips against his, grinding her clit along the length of his cock.

"I want to fuck your ass," he told her, never breaking the eye contact. "Have you ever had your ass fucked, baby?"

"No."

Her response was immediate, and he saw the hesitation flash through her beautiful eyes.

"I need to fuck your ass, baby. Right now." Kane wasn't sure why he needed to take her in such an aggressive, primal way, but he needed it more than his next breath. Maybe because he needed her to trust him, and by allowing him to take her that way, she would have to. If she said no, he wouldn't push her, and within seconds he'd be buried deep in her pussy.

He hoped she didn't say no.

He sensed that she didn't know what to say, so he chose to give her two options. "I want you to move over to the bed and lie down. It's up to you now as to how this plays out. I want to fuck your ass, but I'll take anything you're willing to give me, baby. It's up to you."

Lucie continued to look up at him as though she needed more encouragement. Kane leaned forward, tilting her head by pulling on her hair so he had better access to her neck. Placing biting kisses along her jaw, he continued until his mouth was level with her ear. "Lie on your stomach if you want me to fuck your ass. Otherwise, lie on your back."

It was as simple and easy as that. The way she continued to rub her pussy along his cock, Kane was quickly getting to the point that he didn't care what they did next as long as he was buried inside of her. Releasing the grip on her hair, he took one step back, then another. Lucie's soft, persistent moan was almost the death of him, and when she turned toward the bed, he just stood back and watched.

She climbed onto the bed on all fours, moving to the center with her beautiful ass facing him, the swollen pink folds of her pussy visible between her legs. Just when he thought she would turn over onto her back, she stilled, resting her upper body on her forearms, her head pressing into the mattress.

Kane's heart soared nearly out of his chest. The woman trusted him not to hurt her, although she had never done this before. Moving closer to the bed, Kane opened the drawer of the nightstand and pulled out the bottle of lubrication he had deposited there earlier.

"Move back toward me," he instructed as he flipped open the cap.

When Lucie did as he told her, Kane moved forward, pushing her legs wider so that he could maneuver between them. Brushing his stomach over the backs of her thighs, he placed one hand on her back, forcing her upper body deeper into the mattress.

Leaning forward, he nipped the firm, supple skin of her ass cheek with his teeth, feeling the way Lucie flinched beneath him. Separating the firm globes with his fingers, Kane trailed his tongue over her lower back, down the crease of her ass, until he found the tiny, delicate hole that he was looking for. Gently he began reaming her with his tongue, reveling in her soft moans and the way she began thrusting back against his mouth.

He teased her like that for long minutes before standing once more and grabbing the lubrication from the bedside table. Holding one hand on her hip, he squeezed the lube down the crease of her ass. The shiver that moved through Lucie had Kane's cock jerking.

Fuck! He wanted to slide deep inside of her, but he knew he'd hurt her if he didn't prepare her first. Using one finger, he teased the puckered hole, sliding the lubrication around before slipping the tip of his finger inside of her.

"Let me know if it's too much, Lucie," Kane growled, barely holding on to his control.

Gently, he fingered her ass with one finger, the fingers of his other hand digging into the soft flesh of her hip.

"You're so fucking hot," he groaned before sliding two fingers into her ass, easing them in slow, then retreating. He didn't move quickly, knowing there was no need to rush, no matter how hard his cock was or how damn tempted he was to slam inside of her.

Lucie began thrusting her hips back against his intruding fingers, moaning his name over and over as she did. He knew the pleasure had overtaken some of the pain, but there was still no way he'd fit inside of her without hurting her, so he kept fingering her ass as he leaned forward, peppering her back with open-mouthed kisses.

"I want to bury my cock in your ass, Lucie." Kane kept up a verbal litany of things he wanted to do to her, listening to her moans increase as he began scissoring two fingers inside of her, before inserting a third.

"Kane!" Lucie whimpered, and he stilled. "Oh, God! Don't stop! Please don't stop!"

A growl tore from his chest as he began thrusting three fingers in her ass, deeper with each punishing drive, until he couldn't hold back any longer. Pulling his fingers free, Kane quickly lubed his cock before moving her up on the bed as he climbed onto the mattress on his knees.

With the hand he had holding her hip, Kane leaned into her, finding her clit with his fingers. When she began moaning his name again, he aligned his cock with her tight hole before pressing the swollen head against her, watching as he slipped inside. A torturous groan erupted from his chest as her body enveloped him, strangling the head of his dick.

"Bear down on me, Lucie," he commanded, trying to force his fingers to continue moving over her clit, trying to keep her hovering on the edge and not aware of the pain he knew he was inflicting.

When Lucie pushed back against him, Kane slid farther in, one inch at a time, until he was sweating profusely and his cock was buried to the root inside of her. He didn't move, not wanting to hurt her as she whimpered.

He increased the speed of his fingers over her clit, finding the slick entrance to her pussy with his thumb before pressing into her. She was so fucking tight and so damn hot. He wasn't going to be able to last long.

Pulling back, gripping her hips with both hands, Kane focused on sliding in and out of her hot, smooth channel, over and over.

"Play with your clit, Lucie," he told her when the sweat began sliding down his forehead. He needed to fuck her.

When she moved her hand between her legs, he could only assume she was doing as he'd instructed while he continued to maintain a steady, gentle pace, until Lucie was once again thrusting back against him.

"Fuck me, Kane! Please fuck me," she cried out, trying to force her hips closer to him. With his hands holding her still, she didn't get very far, and he was still scared of hurting her.

"Dammit, Kane!" Lucie screamed, but it wasn't from the pain. "Fuck me now!"

Kane lost his leash on his control, and he began slamming against her, burying his cock to the hilt in her ass, holding her hips and pulling her against him as he pounded into her over and over, faster and harder, until the tingling in the base of his spine robbed him of breath.

"I'm coming!" Lucie's voice broke through the haze that he was trapped in as he tried to hold on until she found her release, but the moment the words penetrated his brain, Kane stilled, spilling himself deep into her.

He didn't know how it was possible, but the woman continued to intensify his feelings for her as every single minute passed.

"I DON'T NEED a bath," Lucie groaned when Kane tried to help her from the bed. She didn't want a bath; she just wanted to close her eyes and give in to the exhaustion pulling at her.

She'd never experienced the kind of mind-numbing orgasm as she'd had moments before. Nor had she expected to come at all from being fucked like that, but clearly she'd shattered into a million pieces thanks to the most body-rocking release she had ever known.

"You're going to be sore," he whispered as he lifted her into his arms and carried her to the bathroom a few minutes later.

At some point, he must have come into the bathroom and filled the tub, because the water was deep, there were mounds of soft, fluffy white bubbles, and the gentle hum of the jets rumbled. Kane placed her on her feet in front of the oversized spa tub, allowing her to climb in first. He kept his hand on her arm until he was in the tub with her, lowering himself behind her.

Lucie slid into the warm water, her eyes closing momentarily as she leaned into Kane, letting the heat from his body mixed with the perfect temperature of the water soothe her aching muscles.

"I'm in awe of you," Kane said long moments later, just when Lucie was beginning to drift into that state of euphoric slumber.

She turned her head to the side and forced her eyes open. "Why?" she asked, unsure what he meant by his comment.

"You amaze me."

"Here I was thinking I was the one being amazed by you," she said lightly.

"After everything I put you through, to know that you trust me... It humbles me, Lucie," he said, his voice sounding somewhat sad.

"I've never had an issue with trust where you're concerned. I know you would never hurt me," she answered, using her hand to swirl circles in the mounds of bubbles across her chest.

"But I did."

Lucie abruptly turned, but Kane easily stopped her, pulling her back against his chest and pressing his lips on the back of her head.

"You didn't hurt me, Kane."

She could understand why he would think that, because she had done the unthinkable, hiding her pregnancy from him and never telling him he was Haley's father. But it never had been about trust. She knew that no matter how many times she tried to explain that to him, he wasn't going to accept it.

"I've dreamt about you," Kane began, his voice low, his hands firm across her abdomen. "After what you told me this morning, I realized they weren't dreams. They were memories, although they always seemed just a little out of reach. I never could completely see what happened, but now I know. I wish it could've been different between us that night."

Lucie didn't respond, unsure what even to say to that. There were so many times that she had wished the same thing. Not about the events of the night, because, if she were honest, she didn't want to change the way that it had happened. She just wished he had remembered so she hadn't had to spend the next five years wondering why it hadn't been good enough for him to remember.

"That was a really dark time for me," Kane explained. "I'm not sure why that year was harder on me than the others, but I had a difficult time dealing with the anniversary of my brother's death."

Lucie didn't move a muscle. Hell, she wasn't even sure she was breathing. Her heart cracked wide open from the sadness she heard in his tone. She waited patiently for him to continue, trying not to disrupt whatever it was that caused him to open up to her. She'd had no idea Kane even had a brother, much less that he had died.

"It would've been his twenty-first birthday that year, and drowning myself in alcohol was the only way I knew to deal with the overwhelming loss that I felt."

Lucie thought back to that night and the days preceding it. Kane had been indulging quite a bit more than he normally did from what she remembered. In fact, these days, she rarely saw him drink anything more than a beer. She hadn't thought anything of it.

"How did he die?" she asked, immediately wishing she had kept her mouth shut. Kane didn't move, nor did he answer her for several seconds, or maybe it was minutes. Lucie wasn't sure, but she didn't breathe during that time.

"Drunk driver." Those two words broke through the otherwise silent bathroom, aside from the gentle hum of the motor from the tub jets.

"Oh, Kane." Lucie's heart leapt into her throat. "I'm so sorry."

"He was the drunk driver," Kane stated firmly, his tone no longer sad.

Lucie detected the underlying anger mingling with the agony she imagined he felt. "He was only sixteen years old, for chrissakes! He was so damn smart; it still boggles my mind why he would do something so stupid."

Lucie couldn't help but think back to that night when she had driven Kane home from the club. Had she not intervened, she knew he would've gotten behind the wheel drunk. She didn't want to think about what might've happened if she hadn't been there to stop him.

"Thankfully no one else was hurt. He wrapped his car around a tree. They said he was killed instantly and that his blood alcohol level was more than triple the legal limit."

*Captivated*

Lucie's heart went out to Kane and his mother for what they'd had to go through. She was saddened by the fact that Haley would never get to meet her uncle. Kane's loss explained so much about that night and the way he had treated her. Still, she didn't see it the same way he did. He hadn't hurt her, and never once had she thought he would.

"I love you, Kane," Lucie said quietly after several long, silent minutes. She hadn't expected to say the words aloud, although her heart was consumed with the love she felt for him.

Kane still didn't move, but she was almost positive she felt his hands tighten against her stomach.

Maybe it was too soon for her to say the words, but she couldn't take them back now. She didn't want to. Even if he didn't feel the same for her, Lucie needed him to know just what he meant to her. After Haley had surprised them both by calling him Daddy earlier in the evening, she was pretty sure he was overwhelmed enough already. Thinking about his brother probably didn't help, either.

At least that's what she was going to tell herself. There was no way she could accept that he didn't feel the same for her. Not until she got home, where she would be able to fall apart without him looking on.

# Chapter *Eleven*

THE NEXT FEW days flew by without incident. Kane, Haley, and Lucie spent their days down at the beach, soaking up the sun. He even managed to coax Haley into the water a time or two, although it was obvious his daughter wasn't a water lover like he was. The highlight of the week, though, had been the whale-watching tour. He wasn't sure who had been more excited, Haley or Lucie.

They were on their last full day of their vacation, and Kane had a surprise for Lucie. Any minute now, his mother was going to arrive to spend the day with her granddaughter, which meant he had the opportunity to spend some alone time with Lucie.

After the first night they were there, Kane had been on emotional overload. Between Haley calling him Daddy, which she continued to do every time she spoke to him, making him beam with pride without even knowing it, and Lucie telling him she loved him, Kane was beside himself. Overwhelmed with so much love for these two girls he had come to claim as his own.

Only he hadn't told Lucie that he loved her. He'd been too shocked to speak, never expecting to hear her say the words. She hadn't said anything since, and he knew that was because he had so easily ignored the situation, trying selfishly to come to terms with how he could explain his feelings for her.

Today he was going to have the chance. There was no way he was going to let another day go by without showing Lucie exactly how much she meant to him.

The gentle knock on the condo door had both Haley and Lucie turning abruptly to look at him. He smiled and moved over to the door. A quick glance through the security hole told him it was, in fact, his mother.

After a quick hello, Susanna Steele moved into the living area, followed by a little-girl squeal as Haley recognized who had come to see her.

"Grammy!" Haley yelled as she ran across the room, right into his mother's open arms.

"There's my little ray of sunshine!" Susanna greeted Haley before standing up and facing Lucie. "Hi, honey. You look like you've gotten some sun. You're radiant."

Kane watched the blush creep across Lucie's sun-kissed cheeks, and he smiled. Although Susanna and Lucie had only met one other time, he knew his mother didn't hold anything against her for what she'd done. Susanna wasn't like that. Maybe that's because she had experienced so much pain in her life already, she was constantly reminding him to keep a positive outlook. He wished it had always been that uncomplicated for him.

Kane met Lucie's gaze, and he smiled. Yes, his mother's arrival was obviously a surprise to her, but he had wanted it to be. Seriously, they were in Hawaii of all places, and there was no way he would forgo a relaxing, romantic day with her if he was given the chance. Considering his mother had offered, insisting she wanted to come to Hawaii for a few days anyway — a lie, he knew — he had been unable to refuse her.

"Can we go to the beach, Grammy?" Haley asked, making all of the adults turn to look at her.

"Of course we can." Susanna smiled.

"Will Mommy and Daddy go with us?" Haley asked, and Kane noticed the way his mother's back stiffened. He beamed with pride once more.

Susanna turned and grinned, making him feel even more elated by his daughter's acceptance. When she crouched low, getting right at eye level with Haley, Kane waited to hear what she was going to say next.

"Don't tell anyone," Susanna said in a mock whisper, "but I think your daddy is going to take your mommy on a date."

Kane met Lucie's gaze again, and he saw the smile tip the corners of her perfect heart-shaped lips. He was happy to know she was on board with the plan.

An hour later, Kane was assisting Lucie off of the small speedboat that had transported them from Maui to a small, quaint island that the natives boasted about. According to what he had heard, there was a tiny resort that had beachfront rooms, and lucky for him, they had had a vacancy when he'd called. Considering they were flying back home the following afternoon, he had reserved it for their last night there with the understanding that Susanna would be staying with Haley overnight.

Lucie hadn't complained, but nor had she said anything else since they'd left the condo. He'd tried for small talk, but the most he could get out of her were brief yes or no answers.

After a short trek from the beach up to the small cluster of individual cottage-style structures, Kane found the number of the room they had been assigned to. With him carrying the one bag they had packed containing both of their things for one night, they moved along the walkway until they reached the semi-private condo.

Looking around, he admired the view of the beach and the numerous palm trees that waved back and forth in the gentle breeze. This was perfect for what he had in mind.

After opening the door with the key he had been given earlier on the main island, he entered the small bungalow and stepped back so that Lucie could join him. Once inside, he admired the cozy, elegant surroundings before dropping the bag at his feet.

"You really didn't have to go to all this trouble," Lucie stated, standing in the middle of the room, her arms crossed over her midsection like she was keeping herself warm. Kane knew that wasn't the case, because without so much as a breeze, the room was stifling.

Moving around to the windows, he pushed them open, allowing the warm breeze to circulate through, stirring the sheer curtains. Once that was done, he crossed over to where she stood, pulling her up against him. Ever since the night Lucie had told him that she loved him, Kane knew he'd been a little standoffish.

He'd even resorted to sleeping on the couch after they'd made love because she had insisted she was going to do so. After their bodies had come together, something neither of them could resist no matter how awkward things had become between them, they had both fallen fast asleep until Haley had woken them each morning ready to go back to the beach.

Now, they had their own beach, and it was high time Kane gave Lucie some of the attention she deserved. "Do you want to go for a swim? Or for a walk?" he asked when she didn't move to get closer to him.

"It doesn't matter."

"Okay, then. Get changed," he instructed before letting her go and grabbing their bag. After retrieving their bathing suits, he set hers on the bed and then quickly disrobed, pulling on his board shorts, forgoing a T-shirt. The way her eyes slid over his skin as he did made Kane's cock twitch, eager and ready for her attention.

It was clear that was the last thing on her mind, so he simply turned and walked out onto the deck that overlooked the ocean while he waited for her.

Lucie had no idea what was going on, and her mind was still a whirlwind of activity. It had been ever since Susanna Steele had walked into their condo, a huge smile on her face and open arms for her granddaughter.

Now, here she was on a secluded island with Kane for at least the next twenty-four hours, and she wasn't sure what he expected from her. Since the first night they were there, things hadn't been the same. Ever since she had made the compelling mistake of telling him that she loved him.

Although she fully intended to wait until she got back home to Texas to break down into a sob fest the likes of which she had never known before, Lucie was having a difficult time remembering that. Each night, as she lay in bed alone, she'd cried herself to sleep, albeit silently.

And now here she was on the last day of their vacation without the distraction of Haley to keep her preoccupied. Instead, she was alone with Kane and her own thoughts.

Grabbing her bikini, Lucie ventured toward what she suspected was the bathroom to change. A few minutes later, she emerged, her face washed, and if she was lucky, her eyes weren't too red after the sudden and unfortunate breakdown she'd had while changing. She hadn't been able to stop the tears once they'd started, and now she felt like an idiot yet again.

Moving through the cozy room, she found Kane standing on the deck overlooking the ocean. The same place he had been when she had disappeared into the bathroom. His back was to her, and she took a moment to admire the view. The man was breathtaking with all of that gloriously tanned skin, those sleek muscles on his upper back, his lean, slim waist, and his perfect ass. Lucie was pretty sure they had never made another man as perfect as Kane Steele.

She took a deep breath and moved forward, reciting the pep talk she'd given herself in the bathroom. At least for the next twenty-four hours, she was going to enjoy her time with him. Even if this was all just a fairy tale, Lucie knew she'd never have the same opportunity again. For once in her life, she didn't want to let a moment slip away because, if nothing else, she could file the memory so that she could refer to it on those dark, lonely nights.

When she stepped out onto the deck, Kane turned to face her, taking her hand in his, and then headed down the short steps that led to the most beautiful beach she had ever seen. The one at their condo was lovely, but this one boasted white sand and deep, cobalt-blue waters that made her wish they had more time to enjoy it.

They made it to the water's edge, and Kane turned to face her, tilting her head up so that she had to meet his eyes. Luckily, she had donned her sunglasses, hoping to hide her bloodshot eyes. The last thing she wanted to do was to ruin his vacation. After all, he'd gone through a lot of trouble to make sure she and Haley had an incredible time.

To her surprise, Kane didn't say a word. Instead, he turned back to the brilliant blue sky and led her farther in until they were both waist deep. At that point, he turned and grabbed her, pulling her close and surprising the breath right out of her. When he pulled her down on top of him, Lucie was unable to remain on her feet, so she stumbled into the ocean. Somehow Kane managed to keep her head above the water and wrap her legs around his waist at the same time.

"Are you okay?" he asked, pulling her sunglasses from her face.

Lucie immediately turned away, looking farther out into the ocean and wishing, for a minute, that the water would just swallow her up. She was going to ruin this trip for him, and the last thing she wanted to do was to disappoint him one more time. Before he had a chance to get a good look at her eyes, Lucie crushed her mouth to his, wrapping her arms around his neck and lacing her fingers in his soft, wet hair.

Kane groaned into the kiss, his tongue dueling with hers as though he knew as well as she did just how short-lived their romance was going to be. Once they were back in the real world, they were going to have to come to an agreement on how they would co-parent Haley, because it was clear that he didn't have the same feelings for her that she did for him.

Not that she blamed him.

There was a sharp bite of pain in her scalp when Kane pulled her head back by her hair, nipping her neck, before pinning her with those steel-gray eyes.

"I need to be inside of you, Lucie."

The urgency in his tone was unmistakable, making her body tremble despite the warmth of the sun beating down on her skin and the heat of the man pressed against her.

"God, yes," she groaned, crushing her mouth to his in order to ensure she didn't do something stupid. Like break down in tears again.

Kane let go of her hair, reaching beneath the water and pushing down his shorts before pulling her bikini bottoms to the side. Without warning, the tip of his cock breached her swollen, aching entrance, and in one thrust, he was buried to the hilt inside of her.

Lucie was panting already, on the verge of begging him to fuck her because she needed something to distract her from her thoughts. Being filled by him was one of the most serene feelings she had ever known, and it didn't matter whether he was taking her sweetly or they were fucking like rabbits. No matter how he took her, when Kane was inside of her, Lucie knew she would never belong to another man again.

"God, you're so tight," Kane growled in her ear, holding her as tightly as she was holding him. He continued to move farther out into the ocean until he could stand at his full height and they were submerged up to their necks in the water.

The buoyancy of the water didn't allow him to thrust as hard as she wanted him to, but their bodies found a rhythm that matched the pounding of her heart. Lucie felt her impending orgasm as the tingling began deep and slow, but before she could push herself over, Kane stilled.

"Please fuck me," she begged, trying to bury her face in his neck so he didn't see the tears that she was unable to control.

"Let me love you, Lucie," he whispered, and a sob wracked her entire body.

Those were the words she had longed to hear from him, but she knew he didn't mean them in the same context her heart wanted him to.

Lucie began rocking against him, trying to force him deeper, until Kane took over, thrusting into her until her orgasm was in reach once more.

"Come for me, Lucie," Kane whispered as he nipped her earlobe, one hand snaking between their bodies until his thumb was pressing against her clit, rubbing circles until she exploded. His mouth found hers as her body shook, his release not far behind.

# Chapter *Twelve*

BEING BACK AT the club after seven days in paradise with the two girls he loved more than life itself proved harder on Kane than he'd expected. They arrived back in Dallas late on Sunday evening, and after dropping Lucie and Haley off at her apartment, he'd found it difficult to go home to an empty house. Having spent every day with them, he found the quiet lonelier than ever before.

But that wasn't the case at the club. The place was jumping, the crowd bigger than he expected on a Monday night, but apparently that was to be expected when Luke McCoy, owner of Club Destiny, chose to close the doors on the mysterious swingers' club. He hadn't closed the door on the nightclub that allowed the general public admission, and that was evident.

People were coming from all over just to see what the fuss was about. Kane had known before he'd disappeared on vacation that there was something going down, mainly because of the arrival of McKenna Thorne, the reporter for one of Dallas's esteemed swingers' magazines. She had been given provisional entry into the members-only club that even Kane wasn't privy to.

Not that he had ever applied to join. He knew he had the money required, but he had never seen the point in joining. He had enough going on in his life as it was. Especially now that he was trying to come up with a plan to make Lucie his forever.

*Forever.*

It was a term he'd never thought he'd become familiar with, but after the last week, he knew there was no way in hell he was going to allow her to slip through his fingers again. They'd overcome some serious obstacles in the years they had known each other, and as far as he was concerned, the hard part was behind them.

He loved her.

Now he just needed to find a way to tell her. The three little words had been on the tip of his tongue for days, yet he'd been worried that he wouldn't be able to express them well enough. Kane wasn't known for his communication skills.

The sound of the song being butchered by a wannabe karaoke singer had him damn near cringing. What the fuck had Luke been thinking when he'd decided to make Monday nights karaoke night? For the last few months, Kane had endured some of the most gruesome attempts to brutalize a song, and he didn't know how much more he could stand.

Glancing over to the other end of the bar, Kane noticed Lucie talking to someone. The man had his back to the bar so Kane couldn't tell who he was, but he could sense that the conversation wasn't pleasant. It didn't happen often, but from time to time, a drunken guy would take to harassing one of the waitresses. Usually Kane or one of the bouncers could intervene before things got out of hand, which he fully intended to do now.

Lifting the bar top and easing out from behind the bar, Kane left Jacob Heyman, one of the club's few bartenders, to tend to the customers lined up for what seemed like miles.

As he got closer to Lucie and the man she was talking to, or rather arguing with, he realized immediately who it was. Justin Jones. Not the man Kane wanted to see tonight. Or ever, for that matter.

"Is there a problem here?" Kane asked, keeping his voice low and his eyes trained on Justin. He was received with a stern look from Lucie and an easy disregard from Justin. Bastard.

"Why don't you mind your own fucking business," Justin retorted, and Kane could smell the booze on his breath. He was beyond intoxicated.

"She *is* my business," Kane replied, moving to stand directly in front of Justin, crossing his arms over his chest. He easily had a good six inches on Jones and probably at least thirty pounds of solid muscle. Not that the man was scrawny, but Kane knew he could hold his own. He didn't expect it to come to that, though.

"How so?" Justin asked, turning to look at Kane directly. He seemed genuinely interested in knowing just how Kane played into this.

He didn't respond immediately because he wasn't looking to embarrass Lucie, but he needed to get this situation under control and, more importantly, get Justin into a cab before he did something stupid like try to get in his car drunk.

Kane glanced over to see Jacob looking his way, and he nodded his head toward the phone just beneath the bar. The bartender didn't need any more explanation as he picked up the phone and dialed the number taped close by.

"Why don't we take this outside?" Kane asked, and he knew immediately that Justin was going to get all riled up. He had no intention of fighting the man, but he needed to get him outside and on his way.

"I'll go outside, but only if she'll go with me," Justin replied, looking toward Lucie.

Kane waited to see what she would say. When she nodded her head, he held out his arm to allow her to lead the way.

Once outside, Justin did the unthinkable, and Kane could only stand back and stare. The man broke down in tears right there on the sidewalk with probably a good fifty people waiting to get inside. *What the fuck?*

"Please, Lucie," Justin begged, staring at her with tears streaming down his face.

Lucie glanced back at Kane, then turned to face Justin once more, grabbing his arm and leading him a few feet away. The distance between them didn't offer her any more privacy than before, but Kane wasn't about to mention it. If he had to hover over her, he damn sure planned on hearing what she had to say.

LUCIE HAD NO idea what the hell had prompted Justin to show up, begging her to give him another chance. He had never had a chance in the first place. It wasn't like they'd been dating, nor had they ever even been on a date. He just frequently showed up at the club, showered her with attention, which she tried to avoid, and left fairly decent tips.

He'd asked her out a time or two, but Lucie had always politely declined. Just like she had tonight. And yet here they were, standing in front of Club Destiny, the man crying like a baby in front of her while Kane looked on from just a few feet away.

Why did she have to have this conversation in front of Kane? She had already told Justin that she was seeing someone because, well, just because it seemed easier than telling him she wasn't interested. No, she wasn't seeing Kane in the technical sense, and he'd probably laugh if he heard her say it. But with Justin crying and people beginning to gather around them, she needed to put an end to this quickly. She only hoped the cab that Kane had prompted Jacob to call would arrive quickly and save her — and him — from further embarrassment.

"I'm seeing someone, Justin." She repeated the same statement she had given him earlier, only this time she lowered her voice, hoping that Kane wouldn't hear her.

"Who? Who are you seeing?"

Well, so much for trying to be discreet. Lucie couldn't find the words, so she stared back at him, hoping to buy herself a little time.

When Justin moved forward, wrapping his fingers around her arms, Lucie tried to pull back, but his grip was too tight.

"Tell me, Lucie. Who the fuck are you seeing?"

"She's seeing me, asshole. And I'll give you three seconds to get your fucking hands off of her."

Kane's voice was so deep and so low that Lucie barely registered the words he said. It didn't matter what he said, his intentions were clear. To her surprise, Justin immediately released her arms, and Kane pulled her up against his side. When she tried to back away, his hand tightened around her waist, holding her close.

"Get in the cab and go home. You need to sleep it off, man," Kane advised, sounding much more like himself than just moments before.

Justin turned to walk away, but Kane grabbed his arm, releasing his grip on her, and Lucie immediately backed away. That's when she noticed the cab parked at the curb. Kane turned Justin toward the yellow car, opened the back door, and forced him inside. He then leaned in through the front passenger window, talking to the driver, pulling his wallet from his back pocket as he did. Money exchanged hands and then the cab was on its way.

Kane turned back to her, took her hand in his, and then led her back inside the loud bar. God, she was beginning to hate karaoke night. If she had more guts, she'd mention as much to Luke McCoy, but she knew she wouldn't.

Once inside, everything resumed as normal without another word between the two of them. Lucie didn't know if Kane was angry with her, but she wasn't going to ask him. If all went well, she'd get through the next three hours, go home, and crawl into bed and resume the crying jag that sleep had finally interrupted last night.

Lucie had just grabbed her purse and was trying to make it across the room without attracting Kane's attention when she heard him call her name from behind the bar. She stopped, turned slowly, and faced him. With about twenty feet between them, she couldn't see his expression clearly, which was just fine with her. She'd embarrassed him enough for one night.

"I'll call you when I get there," she told him before he prompted her.

He nodded his head but didn't say another word, so Lucie turned toward the parking garage, moving as fast as her tired, aching feet would take her.

Fifteen minutes later, she was locking her apartment door behind her, grateful that Haley was with her mother for the night. After having gone an entire week without seeing her granddaughter, Carolyn had insisted that she get to spend some alone time with her only grandchild. Lucie hadn't been able to argue.

Now, she wanted to fall into bed and resume her crying jag while no one was the wiser. Maybe by morning she'd feel human once again, and she would finally be over Kane Steele.

Not that she actually believed that would happen, but she could hope.

She moved to the kitchen, grabbing a diet soda from the refrigerator and a protein bar from the pantry. She leaned against the counter while she ate, trying not to think about all of the events of the night. She still couldn't believe what Kane had told Justin, but then again, she knew he was just trying to diffuse the situation, which he'd done rather well. For the last few hours, she had warned her heart not to get too excited because he hadn't meant the words he'd said.

Still, her stupid, naive heart had hoped.

Tossing the wrapper in the trash can, Lucie downed most of her drink before flipping off the kitchen light. She was moving through the living room when a knock on the front door damn near had her heart jolting from her chest. Slowly, and as quietly as possible, she moved to the door and peeked through the security hole. There, distorted by the oblong shape of the peephole, was Kane looking awkward, yet still handsome.

Lucie quickly unlocked both locks and opened the door, stepping back so he could enter. It was the middle of the night, and she didn't want to piss off her neighbors and have them call the cops on her. Since this was becoming a frequent occurrence, she was surprised it hadn't happened yet.

Once he was inside, she shut the door, locked it, and turned to face him. Thankfully, she hadn't been crying, because she wasn't sure she could face him if she had.

"We need to talk," Kane said, thrusting one hand through his hair in that adorable way he did as he stared back at her. He seemed irritated. Or maybe he was just concerned. She had no idea.

"About?" she asked because she had no idea where this could possibly be going.

"Is Haley here?"

"No, she's at my mother's."

"Mind if I take a shower?" he asked, and Lucie had no idea what to say. Hadn't he just said they needed to talk? Now he wanted to take a shower? She was confused, but she nodded her head anyway.

Kane disappeared down the short hallway, the bathroom door closing behind him. God, what she wouldn't give for two bathrooms. She really needed to take a shower because she reeked of cigarettes and beer and the last thing she wanted to do was face Kane while she smelled like a damn brewery.

Ten minutes later, he returned wearing only his jeans, sans his boots, socks, and shirt. Damn, the man looked good. Before Lucie could consider what she wanted to do to him while he stood there half-naked, she excused herself to the bathroom so that she could take her own shower.

It took her a little longer than it had him, but not by much. Had she not spent the last five minutes staring at her reflection in the mirror, trying to prepare herself for whatever he wanted to talk about, they'd probably already be done talking and he would be on his way.

Coming out of the bathroom, the first thing she noticed was that all of the lights in her apartment were off, with the exception of a single lamp on her bedside table. The soft golden glow spilled out into the hallway, and Lucie steeled herself for what she would find when she entered her room.

Forcing her feet to move, she walked into her cramped little room, noticing Kane lying on her bed, one arm propped over his eyes. He was still wearing his jeans, but he hadn't bothered to pull down the comforter on her bed.

Was he asleep?

Moving to the opposite side of the bed, Lucie stared down at him, wondering just what the hell she was supposed to do now. Before she could contemplate her next move, Kane raised his arm and looked up at her.

"Lie down beside me."

His voice was gruff from sleep, and she knew he had actually passed out right there in her bed. Instead of arguing, she climbed onto the bed beside him, not pulling the blankets back before she placed her head on the pillow, staring up at the ceiling.

When the lamp turned off, she turned her head toward him but couldn't see a thing in the darkened room.

"Come here, Lucie."

As though she were on autopilot and his voice was her command, her body moved toward him, curling into him as she rested her head on his arm.

"I missed this last night," he whispered into the darkened room, his breath fanning her hair as he spoke the words close to her face.

It wasn't like they had slept in the same bed for the last week, because he had always ventured out to the sofa at the condo while she remained in the bedroom. Lucie hadn't had the luxury of waking up in his arms, and she wondered whether she ever would.

While she had been in the shower, she had resigned herself to listening to everything he had to say. She wasn't going to argue, nor was she going to beg. Instead, she had decided that she would take what he could give her. If that meant he came over and they stole a few hours alone in the dark in her bed each night, so be it. It was more than she felt she deserved.

"We're moving," she blurted out before she thought better of it. Clearly she had an issue with the silence, because she felt the need to fill it with random thoughts.

"Moving?"

"Yes. I found a nicer apartment, and it's in a great neighborhood with good schools. I've been saving up so that Haley and I could move before she started kindergarten."

Kane didn't say anything more; he just pulled her closer, and Lucie listened to the sound of his heart beating beneath her ear. After a few minutes of silence, she figured he'd fallen back asleep. She knew she should try to sleep, too.

"I love you."

Even with the complete silence, Kane's words were barely audible, but Lucie figured that was because her heart had begun to pound like she'd just run a marathon. He didn't move, and he didn't say anything more. She was beginning to think she had imagined it, when finally he repeated the words.

"I love you, Lucie. I've loved you for a long time."

Lucie's fingers dug into the warm skin beneath her fingertips as a single tear slid down her cheek, landing on his chest.

"Don't cry, baby," Kane whispered, pushing her off of him as he maneuvered so that he was above her, resting on his arm.

Lucie couldn't see his face in the dark, but she could feel his presence above her and the weight of his body against her side. She had no idea what to say. She didn't know if her voice would even work, because there was a lump the size of a basketball in her throat.

"I'm sorry I didn't say it before," Kane began, but Lucie immediately silenced him by pressing her fingers against his lips.

"Please don't apologize, Kane. If anyone should say they're sorry, it should be me." She'd hurt him so badly by keeping her secret, and Lucie considered herself lucky that he would even speak to her, much less tell her that he loved her.

"I don't want you to be sorry, either," Kane whispered, his breath closer to her mouth. "I just want you to love me back. I want you to love me forever, Lucie." His mouth pressed gently against hers. "Please just love me forever."

Lucie peered up at him, trying her best to see him in the dark. Her eyes had finally adjusted somewhat, and she could see his profile, but not the pained look she sensed on his handsome face. "I already love you, Kane. And you don't have to worry about forever; I can't go back now. I've never been able to go back."

Kane's warm hands came up and cupped her face, his mouth insistently pressing against hers, his tongue sliding through her lips until she opened wider, letting him in. Letting all of him in.

# Chapter *Thirteen*

KANE ROLLED OVER onto his back, pulling Lucie along with him so that she was perched on top of him, her breasts crushed against his chest, her mouth melded with his. His hands roamed down her sides, gliding over the rounded curves of her breasts, her ribs, her waist, then over her sweet ass covered in a soft, loose material. Boxer shorts? He gripped her ass firmly, pressing her against his insistent, throbbing cock, wanting to feel smooth, hot skin against his.

Having gone without her the night before, Kane felt as though he'd been deprived of her sweetness for a lifetime. Now that he was with her, holding her, kissing her, he knew there was no chance he was ever letting her go again.

When she pulled back, he could see the outline of her face staring down at him. "Make love to me," she whispered into the darkness, and his heart jolted in his chest. He wanted nothing more than to express what this woman made him feel, and the easiest way to do that was when their bodies came together.

Gripping the hem of her tank top, Kane lifted until he could feel the softness of her breasts against his chest. Sliding his hands down the gentle curve of her spine, he slipped them into the shorts she had on, pushing them down over the rounded globes of her ass, down her thighs, until she managed to push them off with her feet.

Now the only thing between them was his jeans. When Lucie moved, taking her warmth with her, he realized what she was doing. With deft movements, she managed to unbutton and unzip him before sliding the denim down his hips. He tried not to hurry, although the desperate need to be inside of her, to hold her to him, was overwhelming.

Once her body was again flush with his, Kane gripped her hips, grinding his erection between her warm, wet folds. "You're wet," he told her as he tilted his head while she placed scorching-hot kisses against his neck. God, the woman was driving him insane.

"Turn around," he demanded, and he felt her hesitation, knew she was questioning his motives. He needed to taste her, to inhale her sweet, musky scent and devour her.

Lucie pushed up to her knees and then climbed over him, but she stopped as she knelt beside him.

"Put your pussy on my mouth," he instructed, wondering what her reaction was going to be. He wasn't fond of the dark, wished like hell he'd left the light on so that he could see her, but this way he'd be able to feel her.

When she straddled his chest, her bottom close to his face, he slid his arms beneath her legs and pulled her hips backward until her sweetness was perched above his mouth. Without hesitation, he pulled her down so that his mouth was buried in her pussy, his tongue sliding between the slick folds until he found her clit.

"Awww, fuck!" Kane damn near came up off the mattress when Lucie took his cock into her mouth, sucking feverishly as she bathed his dick with heat. Trying to focus solely on her, he once again sought her clit with his tongue, circling slowly at first, then increasing the pressure and speed as she returned the favor with her mouth.

The position they were in was too much; she was zapping his concentration with her wicked mouth, and those subtle moans were sending jarring vibrations to his balls. He wasn't ready to come. Not until he was inside of her. But fuck, it felt so damn good.

Blocking out the intense sensations, Kane speared her pussy with his tongue, driving as deep as he could until Lucie was rocking her hips against his mouth, her moans increasing, and now her hand was stroking his cock in a rhythm that matched her soft, warm mouth.

Fuck, he wasn't going to last like this.

In one gentle motion, he managed to flip them so that he was on top, where he could get a better handle on the situation. He needed the control or this woman was going to send him into hyperspace. He fully intended to get there, but not until she was going right along with him.

Turning, he was once again on top of her, their heads at the foot of the bed, his body covering hers. The head of his cock pressed against her warm, wet opening, and he paused.

As their lips touched, their tongues twined together in a deep, soul-wrenching kiss, Kane slid inside of her, the walls of her sex closing around his dick, scalding him with her heat. It was the only place he ever wanted to be. Right here, with this woman, buried inside of her until there was no way to decipher that they were two.

Instead, they were one at this moment. One for always.

He began rocking his hips slowly, going deep, then pulling back. Going deeper with each shallow thrust of his hips. Continuing the motion over and over, Kane tried to keep it slow, to show Lucie just what she did to him. She made him soar, she made his heart pound, and most importantly, she made him feel things he never thought he'd feel.

Complete.

This woman completed him in ways he'd never expected.

"Love me, Lucie," he pleaded with her. Going slow was the only way he knew to show her just what it meant to him to have her like this. Savoring every movement, feeling every gentle plunge of his cock into her depths.

"I'll love you forever, Kane," she whispered back, her fingers sliding into his hair, gripping it harder than he expected. "But now I want all of you. No holding back."

Kane knew what she was saying. Lucie accepted him for who he was. All that he was. This gentle lovemaking was foreign to him, but that didn't mean he didn't want it. There'd be plenty of time for more, plenty of time to take her in all of the ways he had dreamed. But right now, this was perfection.

"I'm not holding back, baby. Not this time." And it was the truth.

Kane began driving into her harder, but never separating their bodies. He closed his mouth over hers, penetrating her deeper with his hips and his tongue at the same time until they were panting, sweat beading on his forehead.

"Oh, God, Lucie. You don't know what you do to me, baby."

"Show me," she murmured against his mouth. "Show me, Kane. Come for me."

Kane pulled back, slammed into her once, twice, until he felt the walls of her sex clenching around his cock, her muscles tightening, her legs wrapped around his hips while her heels pressed into his ass. Leaning up on his forearms, he stared down at her, knowing they couldn't see one another with their eyes, but that didn't matter. Their hearts were all that mattered right then, and when she squeezed him tightly, Kane slammed into her one final time as she screamed his name, pulling his release from him in a rush as she came around his cock.

He wasn't sure whether he deserved a woman as perfect for him as Lucie, and despite her flaws — and his — Kane knew they were meant for each other. It'd just taken a long time to get to this point. But now that they were here, there was no way he was letting her go.

Not ever again.

LUCIE LAY IN the dimly lit room, running her fingers through Kane's silky dark hair as his head rested against her chest. He was heavy, but the weight of him had never felt quite so good. Knowing that he was right there with her, holding her made her heart sigh in relief. This was what she had always longed for.

The way their bodies spoke to one another was unlike anything Lucie had ever known. But the way their hearts connected was more than she felt she deserved. She was flawed; she knew that. She'd made mistakes in her past, and she was pretty sure she'd make more in her future. She wasn't perfect. Neither was Kane. And as far as she was concerned, there had never been two people better suited for one another than the two of them. After all, look what happened when two flawed, imperfect people came together. They created perfection. And her name was Haley.

"Marry me," Kane breathed out roughly, lifting his head from her chest. The early-morning sun was peeking in through the small window in her bedroom, and she could see his face clearly now. What she saw there stole her breath.

Lucie had no idea what to say. Well, that wasn't entirely true. She knew what to say. Yes. It was the only answer if he actually was asking a question. She didn't respond, her brain working feverishly to determine whether her ears had actually heard him correctly.

"Lucie, marry me," he repeated. "Marry me and let's make more perfect babies together. I want to spend my life with you. I want to fall into bed with you each night and wake up with you each day."

She definitely couldn't have imagined that. Lucie felt the smile that split her face, the ray of sunshine that penetrated her heart. "Yes," she whispered, the word barely escaping. "Yes, Kane. Yes, I'll marry you." That time they came out more easily, and she knew at that moment that the smile was now permanent.

"I love you, Lucie. Forever and always, I love you."

"I love you, too, Kane. Now and forever."

# Chapter *Fourteen*

"YOU WANTED TO see me?" Kane questioned Luke as he made his way through the office door.

"Shut the door, please," Luke replied, not bothering to look up from his computer.

Kane closed the door behind him, then moved to a single chair sitting opposite Luke's large desk.

While his boss continued with what he was working on, Kane admired the changes to the office. Before Luke had met Sierra, his office had been just short of a supply closet, although some designer had attempted to give it a personable feel but had only managed to make it worse. If that had even been possible.

Now, the office seemed larger, partly due to the large window overlooking the entire main floor of the club that had been added at Sierra's request. Definitely an improvement. But, then again, there'd been quite a few improvements to Luke since he'd begun sharing his life with Sierra and Cole.

"I wanted to talk to you about your job," Luke stated, looking rather grim and making Kane panic somewhat.

His job? Hell, this couldn't have been about his vacation, could it? He hadn't taken any time off for almost four years, until his recent trip to Hawaii. Surely Luke wasn't upset about that.

"All right." Kane wasn't sure where this was leading, but he was getting more and more anxious the longer Luke stalled.

"I think your time as the bar manager has run its course, don't you?"

What. The. Fuck.

Kane stared back at Luke as confusion and, more importantly, fear churned inside of him. "Do you have a problem with the way I manage the bar?"

If Luke had a problem, he'd never once voiced his concerns.

"Not specifically, no."

"What the hell is going on, Luke?"

A mischievous grin tilted Luke's mouth, successfully pissing Kane off. Thankfully, although Luke was his boss and Kane had a high respect for the man, they had developed a fairly close relationship over the years.

"I know you haven't heard everything about what's been going on with the club, but I'm looking to make some changes. And I need someone I trust to take over a few things for me."

That caught Kane's attention. Maybe it meant he wasn't getting canned.

"And that means what for me?" *And Lucie?* Kane didn't ask the second part, but he was just as interested in any changes that might impact his future wife as he was for himself.

"I need someone to manage the membership of my other club," Luke replied.

"No offense, but I don't know what that means. You've got another club?"

"I do. It's actually in this building."

Could a man be any vaguer? Kane couldn't help but wonder as he waited patiently for Luke to enlighten him.

"We've seen too many problems lately, which is why I temporarily shut the doors. Now I've got Trent breathing down my neck. He's not interested in keeping the doors shut for long, and he wants to know what we're going to do. This is the first of the changes I'm looking to implement."

"Who's Trent?"

"Trent Ramsey," Luke answered easily. "He's a silent partner; well, he was silent until recently."

"Trent *Ramsey*?" Kane asked, stupefied. "*The* Trent Ramsey?" *Holy shit.* Was it even possible?

"That'd be the one."

"And you want me to manage the membership of the swingers' club?"

"Well, that and the fetish club."

"What fetish club?" Kane asked, still trying to keep up. He was having difficulty thanks to Luke's evasiveness.

"The Club at Club Destiny." Luke pulled out a folder from the top drawer of his desk and pushed it toward Kane. "We've managed to keep the club out of the media, which is the reason we have the main club. It's safer that way. With the members that we draw, their anonymity is crucial to our success. However, after what we've recently gone through, I've decided to take a different approach to membership. That's where you come in."

Kane read the information in the folder, what little bit that there was, before turning back to look at Luke. "Who will take over my position as bar manager?"

Luke didn't hesitate with his next answer. "Lucie."

Kane stared blankly at his boss. "You want Lucie to manage the bar?"

"You don't think she can handle it?"

"Not at all." That didn't come out right. "I mean, yes, I think she can handle it. She'll probably do a better job than I can. Everyone loves her, and she's one of the hardest-working people I know."

"I figure now that she has you in her life, where you should've been all along," Luke offered, "she'll have a little more time to devote to the club. You'll have the flexibility to make your own hours, work more at home if you'd like, which should allow Haley to see the two of you more often. What do you think?"

Kane wanted to jump up and down and say yes, but he knew he had to talk to Lucie first. He'd made the mistake of talking to Luke for her once before, and he wasn't willing to do it again.

"I think you should talk to her first. Then she and I can discuss our options," Kane answered. "And if she doesn't want to?"

"Will you base your decision on what she wants?" Luke questioned.

"Not necessarily, no. If she doesn't want to manage the bar, that doesn't mean I'm not interested in this opportunity. Just as long as it doesn't affect her job."

"Lucie and I have a strange relationship, I realize that." Luke stated calmly. "I respect her, although I sometimes question her reasoning."

"I'm sure she'd say the same about you." Kane laughed. Luke wasn't known for his rational thinking most of the time.

"I'm sure she would," Luke answered with a laugh of his own. "If you don't mind, ask her to come see me when you get back downstairs. And I'd appreciate you getting back to me quickly on this. Trent is looking to move forward soon. He's a little concerned about the Walkers' resort. He's not willing to be outdone, so I think it's safe to assume there are more changes in the works."

Kane nodded his head in agreement and then left Luke's office. As soon as he saw Lucie by the bar, he told her that Luke wanted to speak with her. She looked a little concerned, but she stood up straight and made her way upstairs.

Kane wasn't sure what was going to happen next, but he knew one thing for sure. This time, the two of them would work together to determine what was best for their future.

He wouldn't want it any other way.

LUCIE WAS STILL reeling from her conversation with Luke by the time her shift was over the following morning. As she waited for Kane to finish with his inventory, she replayed the conversation over and over in her mind and still came up with the same conclusion. This was an amazing opportunity, and she had wanted to jump at the offer as soon as Luke had told her, but she knew she had to talk to Kane first. She'd learned the hard way exactly what it meant to make decisions without thinking them all the way through.

"You ready?"

Lucie took Kane's hand when he offered it, following him out to the garage. They'd started going into work together after she'd agreed to move in with him. Kane had convinced her that it was inevitable, and since she had so many concerns about the neighborhood she had been living in as it was, she couldn't come up with a good excuse to say no. She was pretty sure Erika was much more comfortable going back to Kane's house with Haley, as well.

"So, what did you think about Luke's offer?" Kane asked as they pulled out of the garage.

She smiled over at him, barely able to contain her excitement. Luke hadn't gone into explicit detail about what Kane would be doing, but he'd alluded to the fact that it would be a step in the right direction for him. The way Luke had expressed his trust in Kane had made Lucie beam with pride. He deserved this chance. She just wasn't sure she deserved anything more than what she had at the moment.

Not that she had told Luke as much.

"I think it's a great opportunity for you," she admitted, turning to face out the window once more.

"What about you?" he asked, and Lucie knew he was aware of the offer Luke had given her.

"Do you think I can do it?" She wasn't going to ask whether she deserved it, because she knew Kane wouldn't tell her no.

She had her own doubts, but since she was only interested in doing what was best for Haley, she wasn't going to make decisions based on her own self-doubt. She was moving forward, and the mistakes of her past were just that. She knew she had to overcome them eventually, and dwelling on them didn't help the situation.

"I think you'll be fantastic," Kane said with a smile. "Everyone loves you. You already know everything there is to know about managing the bar as it is."

True. Lucie had been around long enough to know the ins and outs of Kane's job. She'd even backed him up once or twice over the years. She just hadn't thought this was ever even a possibility.

"What did you tell Luke?" Lucie asked, realizing he might've already taken the job.

"I told him he needed to talk to you, and that we'd decide what was best for the three of us at that point."

Lucie's heart swelled to near bursting. After so many speed bumps along the way, it was still hard to believe that she had somehow made it to this point. To have Kane's love was one of the greatest gifts she had ever known. And now that they were working together to raise their daughter, everything just seemed to be as it should be.

Although she'd love to be able to go back and change the way she'd handled things, she knew that no matter how they'd gotten to this point, it was where they were supposed to be. It felt right.

And that's exactly what she told Kane.

The smile he beamed at her made her heart leap with joy. They'd finally done it.

They'd finally managed to secure their happily ever after.

# *Epilogue*

THE WEDDING WENT off without a hitch, but Kane wouldn't have expected anything less. After Lucie's insistence that they only have a few friends and family and, of course, their precious Haley, there hadn't been much room for error.

Not that he had cared who attended. His eyes had been on Lucie from the moment she'd stepped into the small church aisle on the arm of Luke McCoy, a man who, no matter what people thought, wasn't nearly as much of a hard-ass as he let them believe. He'd insisted that he be allowed to walk Lucie down the aisle, and he'd even told Cole that he'd fight him for the honor. Originally, Lucie had asked Cole, but even after he'd agreed, Luke had contacted her personally requesting the honor. Although he knew she had been a little nervous, and even more confused, Lucie had been thrilled with the idea. It meant a lot to her after what she and Luke had gone through the year before.

They had followed Haley, who'd tossed white rose petals along the way, causing smiles and laughter from the small group of people, including Sierra, Cole, Logan, Samantha, and of course, Kane's mother, Susanna, and Lucie's mother, Carolyn.

The day couldn't have been more perfect. Lucie couldn't have been more perfect.

Their flight had been a long one, and they had finally made it to the small Hawaiian island and even managed to get the same cozy bungalow they'd stayed in that one night three months ago.

It was dark, and the only light came from the brilliant moon that sat low on the ocean, casting a bright white glow over everything around them. Lucie had disappeared into the bathroom a few minutes ago, telling him that she needed to change. Kane only hoped she was going to get naked, because he wasn't sure how much longer he could go without getting his hands on her.

When warm hands glided down his back, Kane almost jumped. He hadn't heard her join him. The warmth of her skin against his made him relax instantly. When he started to turn around, Lucie applied pressure to his back, keeping him facing forward. He stopped, not pushing any farther, figuring she had this all planned out.

"See those people down there on the beach?" she asked as she placed a kiss against his back, sending a shiver racing down his spine.

"I see them," he replied. There were four people sitting around a bonfire about fifty yards away.

"You don't want them to hear you, do you?"

Kane smiled. He didn't give a fuck if they heard him or not, but he understood where she was going with this. When her hands wrapped around his waist, her fingers easily unbuttoning his shorts, Kane didn't make a move. Within seconds, he was naked on the deck, the glow of the moon offering anyone within viewing distance an unobstructed view of his body.

"Put your hands on the rail," she instructed, and he smiled at her attempt to sound stern.

Kane placed his hands palms down on the wooden rail that surrounded the small deck. When Lucie gripped his hips, forcing him to move his feet backward, he let her. Because of his height and his long arms, there was plenty of room between him and the railing, which apparently Lucie was planning to utilize, because she maneuvered in front of him, tossing a pillow on the ground and lowering her naked body to her knees.

His breath lodged in his chest as he looked down at her dark hair spilling over her creamy shoulders. Oh, she was a sight to see.

She would be somewhat hidden by the wood slats in the railing, but he wasn't. When she looked up at him and smiled, Kane damn near lost it.

"Don't move your hands from the railing, or I'll stop," she told him, looking serious.

She didn't have to worry. There was no way he was moving from this spot. When she gripped his cock, her silky fingers sliding along the hard length, Kane hissed out a breath.

She was going to kill him before the night was over; he knew it. When her lips wrapped around the engorged head, he suddenly realized that if she did, he couldn't ask for a better way to go.

♥□□□□♥□□□□♥

I hope you enjoyed Kane and Lucie's story. Captivated is #4.5 in Nicole's bestselling Club Destiny series. You can read more about Club Destiny as well as her other series on her website. Did you know that the Club Destiny and Alluring Indulgence series overlap?

You can find the full reading order at:

www.NicoleEdwardsAuthor.com.

Want to see some fun stuff related to my books, you can find extras on my website. Or how about what's coming next? I keep my website updated with the books I'm working on, including the writing progression of what's coming up for my standalone novels. www.NicoleEdwardsAuthor.com

If you're interested in receiving updates on all that I'm working on, you can sign up for my monthly newsletter.

Want a simple, *fast* way to get updates on new releases? You can also sign up for text messaging on my website or simply text NICOLE to 64600 (US only). I promise not to spam your phone. This is just my way of letting you know what's happening because I know you're busy, but if you're anything like me, you always have your phone on you.

And last but certainly not least, if you want to see what's going on with me each week, sign up for my weekly Hot Sheet! It's a short, entertaining weekly update of things going on in my life and that of the team that supports me. We're a little crazy at times and this is a firsthand account of our antics.

# About Nicole

*New York Times* and *USA Today* bestselling author Nicole Edwards lives in Austin, Texas with her husband, their three kids, and four rambunctious dogs. When she's not writing about sexy alpha males, Nicole can often be found with her Kindle in hand or making an attempt to keep the dogs happy. You can find her hanging out on Facebook and interacting with her readers - even when she's supposed to be writing.

Website: NicoleEdwardsAuthor.com

Facebook: Author.Nicole.Edwards

Twitter: @NicoleEAuthor

Nicole also writes contemporary/new adult romance as Timberlyn Scott.

*By Nicole Edwards*

## The Alluring Indulgence Series
*What's hotter than a Texas cowboy? Seven Texas cowboys.*
*All with a heart of gold and a sexy, devious side.*

Kaleb

Zane

Travis

Holidays with the Walker Brothers

Ethan

Braydon

Sawyer

Brendon

## The Club Destiny Series
*Come see how hot these powerful men and their lovely ladies can*
*get. All from the comfort of the infamous Club Destiny.*

Conviction

Temptation

Addicted

Seduction

Infatuation

Captivated

Devotion

Perception

Entrusted

Adored

### The Dead Heat Ranch Series

*Love cowboys? Love smokin' hot cowboys and the sweet, sexy cowgirls they love? Come on in and stay a while.*

Boots Optional

Betting on Grace

Overnight Love

### The Devil's Bend Series

*Sexy is just the beginning for these down home cowboys. Add in a little country music, some big dreams and you're in for a ride.*

Chasing Dreams

Vanishing Dreams

### The Devil's Playground Series

*Come hang out at Devil's Playground - the hottest nightclub in Las Vegas, Dallas and New York! This is a spin-off series from Southern Boy Mafia, featuring those who work at Max Adorite's nightclub, Devil's Playground.*

Without Regret

### The Pier 70 Series

*Who knew a day on the lake could be this hot?*

Reckless

### The Sniper 1 Security Series

*The Kogans and the Trexlers are in the business of protecting those who need to be protected. And their motto is: Protect... by any means necessary.*

Wait for Morning

Never Say Never

**The Southern Boy Mafia Series**
*Everybody loves a bad boy!*

Beautifully Brutal
Beautifully Loyal

**Standalone Novels**
*Just to spice things up a bit!*

A Million Tiny Pieces
Inked on Paper

**Writing as Timberlyn Scott**

Unhinged
Unraveling
Chaos

**Naughty Holidays**

2015

**Because Naughty can be oh so Nice**®

Made in the USA
San Bernardino, CA
13 January 2016